Creations 2014

Ada Writers

ISBN 978-1-304-94167-1

Printed in the United States of America

10 9 8 7 6 5 4 3 2 1

Dedicated to
our families & friends
who support our writing habit.
Thank you.

Contents

Short Stories

Excerpts from Books and Novels in Progress

About the Authors   **119**

Ada Writers is dedicated to the joy of writing and to aiding writers at any level in their ongoing pursuit of writing well. From beginning to experienced writers, we encourage creative activity by publishing this annual anthology. Visit AdaWriters.blogspot.com. Thank you.

A Chicago Valentine
By Martha Rhynes

In February 1929, Alphonse Gabriel "Scarface Al" Capone luxuriated in the sunshine and sea breezes at his winter home in Florida, far from the windswept, cold streets of Chicago. His assistant in crime, Jack "Machine Gun" McGurn, informed him that George "Bugs" Moran's rival gang in Chicago had highjacked a shipment of whiskey. Moran's "Irish" gang was also trying to cut in on the numbers racket, gambling at the dog track, "protection" at speakeasies, brothels, and other lucrative but illegal business ventures in Chicago.

Capone and his powerful gang plotted vengeance and murder. To avoid identification, they hired Egan's Rats, a gang from St. Louis, to assassinate Moran and his gang. Spies discovered Moran's headquarters in a trucking garage. Knowing Moran's gang would be there to unload delivery trucks, Capone's gang made a fake deal to deliver a shipment of prime whiskey from Detroit to the garage on February 14, at 10:30 a.m.

On Valentine's Day, five assassins arrived in a black Cadillac they had equipped to look like a police car. Two of the assassins wore Chicago police uniforms. The other three wore business suits, neckties, and hats. They carried automatic weapons and extra ammunition. Two women in a rooming house across the street observed them and assumed they were law-enforcement officials.

"Bugs" Moran arrived late, but when he saw a police car parked in front of the garage, he drove away. Inside the garage, his gang of seven men were surprised when "policemen" entered, but they concluded: It must be a raid! So they raised their hands, faced the wall, and allowed their weapons to be removed. Then an unexpected rain of bullets annihilated them, leaving a bloody mass of bodies piled against the wall. Only the shop dog, a German shepherd, survived.

The howling dog finally alerted neighbors to call authorities, who found seven bullet-riddled bodies and identified them. Women across the street said they heard gunshots and observed the exit of "policemen" and men whom they assumed were federal agents. They watched them leave in the black Cadillac. Later, they identified several of the assassins from photographs. The license plate on a burned-out Cadillac eventually linked it to a gangster from St. Louis. Two men in the Capone gang were arrested and charged with murder, but evidence was unreliable. One used "the blonde alibi," a perfect excuse, because a blonde wife could not testify against her husband.

Proving Capone was the ringleader of the murders and other crimes was difficult to prosecute because he successfully bribed law-enforcement officials and donated generously to charities. Although he claimed to be "a simple businessman, giving people what they want," he was the "brains" behind criminal activities in Chicago.

His life of crime began during his teens in New York City, where his mentor was a clever Italian gangster, Johnny Torrio. Young Capone loved fancy clothes, so his nickname was "Snorky," that is, until a girlfriend's brother slashed his face with a knife, and his moniker became "Scarface." Always a target for assassination attempts, Capone maintained two bodyguards and a chauffeur.

He was arrested for tax evasion and attempted bribery in 1931, for which he paid fines and spent eight years in prison. The government confiscated his property, including a bulletproof limousine, which President Franklin D. Roosevelt used. Capone died in 1947 from physical and mental disease caused by neurosyphillis. His illegal activities have inspired numerous books, films, and dramas.

SOURCES
Bardsley, Marilyn. "Al Capone: Chicago's Most Infamous Mob Boss" in *Crime Library* @trutv.com
O'Brien, John. "The St. Valentine's Day Massacre" in *Chicago Tribune*. February 14, 1929.
Rosenberg, Jennifer. "St. Valentine's Day Massacre" in *20th Century History* @About.com

Count My Blessings
By Loretta Yin

What is a blessing?
A Boon—something beneficial or pleasant that is bestowed —a blessing.
Bestowed—given to me—by whom?
Come to think of it, no one really bestowed anything to me. Except my parents. They supported me, fed and clothed me, shielded and protected me.

I usually have to work for whatever. I have to earn it. I have worked hard for what I have now. But when it comes to person-to-person relationships, I guess I did not work hard enough to make them smooth sailing sometimes.

I do and count my blessings, however. I am blessed with a good roof over my head, with things that I love surrounding me (art, music, etc., included) with an income enough to keep me fed and clothed and to sustain my indulgences—making art and traveling.

I am blessed with three honest, trustworthy, and hard-working daughters (though stubborn—or should I say strong-willed—a characteristic makes them independent, focused, and reliable), three good sons-in-law. Three wonderful grandchildren. At will, I can do most whatever I wish to do—barring some natural limitations—can't change that. So, accept it.

I have good friends and great neighbors. I have their love and caring, and I believe, their respect.

In spite of the many ups and downs in my life, my life has been relatively peaceful and pleasant.

Hey, I grew up knowing curfews, killings, air-raids, wars, black-market, being refugees.

Miraculously, I had never suffered any physical harshness in life - not even being hungry at any given time.

I, together with my family, was a "citizen of the world," with no country to belong to for a number of years in my younger days. But, there were always lights at the end of the tunnel. There were usually solutions to problems.

Being in a marriage with a husband who had plenty of health problems and a lousy attitude towards life was not easy to say the least. I survived by being "stubborn."

"Pull your socks up."

"Carry on."

You vowed to stick with the person "for better or for worse, in sickness and in health." So be it.

My marriage lasted forty-eight and a half years before I became widowed.

I made my path in my journey of life. I am living a healthy, peaceful, and pleasant life.

I am blessed.

Gray Monday
By James Sanders

This is a gray Monday. There is some ice on the trees and grass but not very much and it is not supposed to last very long.

The trees across the highway are just a shadow almost hidden in the clinging damp grip of the fog.

This is the type of day that could easily give birth and nourishment to mental depression. Or! On the other hand, it could inspire the imagination to greater heights of inventiveness.

For instance, instead of sitting here at the kitchen table staring out at the fog and watching the Blue jays, Cardinals and Sparrows take their turn at the feeders, I could be sitting on a sun-drenched, deserted anti-aircraft gun emplacement atop diamond head in Hawaii. Far below and to my left, sun browned surfers would be zigging and zagging to keep their desired position on the white capped waves. Close to shore, the surfers would quit the wave and paddle back out to catch another. The wave is left to its fate of crashing into the rocks and dying in a blast of spray and to the relentless sound of battle between sea and shore.

Looking out in front of me the ocean is a beautiful blue with patches of green closer to shore. I can also see the dark jagged outline of a reef just below the surface of the water. The reef is sharp and dangerous to bare skin or ships that might stray onto it. But it is beautiful to look at.

Or I could be 10,000 feet up in the Colorado Rockies listening to the wind skip through the treetops, hear a crow somewhere in the valley below calling to its mate or even the bugle call of an elk. I could lay there in the sun zipped up in my coveralls and watch the vapor trails stretch in all directions across the sky. Imagining all kinds of places they could be headed.

I could look out across the mountaintops and valleys and dream of the adventures of hunters, trappers, and rugged pioneers who settled this rugged country.

I could see a deer move quietly into the meadow, head erect, alert and ready to sprint for cover at the slightest hint of danger.

As I lay there without human companionship but surrounded by God's creation, I could smell the fresh, pungent scent of pine. I could feel the sun bathe my face and heart with its warm caress, taste the sweetness of my candy bar as well as life itself, and so it goes on a gray Monday.

His Power In Song
By Kelley Benson

It is sobering to walk thru an old graveyard and realize how nearly everything written on the face of the stones are often illegible. The sobering part is knowing that the person's body that lies beneath your feet was once, perhaps, staring at another stone coming to their own realization of how brief life is, and now who they are is faded and worn, along with whatever mark they left on earth.

James said in James 4:14, *"You do not know what your life will be like tomorrow. You are just a vapor that appears for a little while and then vanishes away."* In your brief, vapor-like life what do you hope will be said about you? Were you courageous? Were you kind, or generous? Did you fight to make a difference for those that couldn't or didn't know how to fight for themselves? Realize this; you will never be any of those things without effort. It takes a conscious thought to be courageous, kind or generous, or compassionate.

When we choose to live beyond our fears, and above reproach we will be persecuted for it in some way or another, but after all the "dust settles," we will be remembered for what really matters. Although it shouldn't be our goal to be remembered for our sakes; but Jesus said in Matthew 5:16, *"Let your light shine before men in such a way that they may see your good works, and glorify your Father who is in heaven."*

Songs have always been a powerful way to express our gratitude for someone. Martin Luther once wrote, "[Music is] a fair and lovely gift of God…next to the Word of God the mistress and governess of the feelings of the human heart." Therefore, it's no surprise that people all throughout the Bible used a song to express their gratitude. And so many of the stories of deliverance were foreshadows of what Christ would offer for each of us in the end.

For instance, when God led the Israelites out of Egyptian slavery, after they crossed thru the Red Sea and their enemies were destroyed, Moses couldn't help but sing about God's power over death. He sang in Exodus 15:2, 13, *"The Lord is my strength and song, and He has become my salvation; this is my God, and I will praise Him; my father's God, and I will extol Him... In Your loving kindness You have led the people whom You have redeemed; in Your strength You have guided them to Your holy habitation."*

They realized how God had turned their day of fear into something amazing—freedom from death. That same sentiment was echoed often throughout the Old Testament as God would perform acts of deliverance from the hands of those that wanted to destroy His people. But a time would come when redemption would come thru Jesus Christ; who would courageously take on death to become the Savior of the world, an act worth praising God about.

What do we sing about today? The people that followed after Christ, and were there at the beginning of the church realized the brevity of life and the need to live to glorify God in all that we do. On several occasions, the apostles experienced beatings and time in prison for being courageous and compassionate towards a lost and dying world by telling them about what Jesus came to do.

In Acts 4:19-21, 24, the apostles told the Sanhedrin, *"'Whether it is right in the sight of God to give heed to you rather than to God, you be the judge; for we cannot stop speaking about what we have seen and heard.' When they had threatened them further, they let them go...because they were all glorifying God for what had happened... [the apostles] lifted their voices to God in unison."* Their courage to trust God opened an opportunity for them to praise God for His goodness, but it also opened an opportunity for those watching, to praise Him as well.

Our songs that we sing have a purpose in expressing what God has done for us here, but especially in what He's going to do after our time on this earth is over. As Paul said in 1 Corinthians 15:54-57, *"Death is swallowed up in victory. O death, where is your victory? O death, where is your sting? The sting of death is sin, and the power of sin is the law; but thanks be to God, who gives us the victory through our Lord Jesus Christ."*

Next time you start to sing a song to God, consider what He's done in your life worth singing about. It's a healthy way to express ourselves to God, but it's one we shouldn't participate in lightly. Come let us sing with joy to the Lord!

Leather Craft
By Mel Hutt

Leather crafting has been a part of my life for many years. It started when I was nearing my retirement from the City of Norfolk, Virginia. I have always enjoyed craftwork in other media and decided to try making some Christmas presents for the family.

My first attempt at carving and tooling leather was a disaster. I had bought a beginner's kit from Tandy leather and tried to follow directions, but to no avail. I went back to the Tandy store and learned that they gave lessons in basic carving and tooling. This was my opportunity to try something new.

Dorothy and I both loved to shop and sell in flea markets, and this new craft was a new challenge in the making. I worked up to being pretty good at the many parts of successful leatherwork, including lacing, carving, and tooling. Belts and wallets were my specialty. This allowed me to personalize the finished product.

I am still using belts and wallets that I crafted nearly twenty years ago. I learned to be especially good at lacing and hand sewing. Of course, it was desire and practice that made my finished product special. I designed two special stamps that I still use today. One was a logo that printed out "Leather is ~~Beather~~ Better." (Beather had the line through it.) Then I had a "Mel's Leather craft" stamp made.

I did not market my belts priced with a buckle as I carried many buckles separately and at various prices and styles. I made a special display for my many belts and would cut to fit tight on the spot using my special measuring belt as a guideline.

The largest width belt I made was four inches wide. It was for a man who called himself Santa Claus. He had me put that in large letters on the back of the belt, and I had a special buckle made for it. He actually had his name changed. He was bearded and would dye his beard white for his role as Santa commercially. He was happy with the results and let people know who made the belt.

Another time I made a belt seventy inches long. The man couldn't get out of his car. I just barely made the length without having to sew an additional length piece.

The biggest selling belt width is usually one and one half inches. Many dress belts are one inch in width. I have made and carved/tooled wider and narrower belts. I have made "money belts," too. I also make them in different colors, though black seems to be the most popular.

As I lack a suitable shop to work in now, I have to limit my work. It is too hot as I write this, and the shop in the barn is too hard to heat for winter use. In Virginia, our living room and dining room were the craft shops as Dorothy is also a crafter.

Crafting is both enjoyable and challenging. It helps me keep my mind working and be productive at the same time.

On Being Eighty-five
By Loretta Yin

Eighty-five.
I'm turning eighty-five next month.
I'm so glad. I have lived long enough to say these words and celebrate their meaning.

I'm alive. I'm healthy.

I no longer have to be concerned with what anyone thinks of me. I'm turning eighty-five and I've earned the right to be ME.

I'm amazed at the way my journey here on earth continues to unfold.

I grew up during some tumultuous political times, but had always had "love and care" from my parents. They sheltered me from the cold and cruel "outside world," and made my life wonderful. In spite of the terror of war, the awful killings around us, and the cruelties of the enemies, of living in constant fear... I learned to entertain myself with rented block-printed storybooks—the adventures of the good-against-evil taught me my life-long lessons. I learned to listen to a few precious 78 long-playing records on a hand-cranked gramophone— the emotion-filled Chinese Classic opera sung in poetry—they gave me my lifelong love of music. My long journey from my birth in Manchuria (the very northern part of China), to Shanghai (the Pearl of the Orient), to Hong Kong (the safe haven for refugees from China; Hong Kong was part of Great Britain at that time), and then to the democratic United States of America...

From a girl in old China to a wife and mother in the U.S., I remained adventurous, and always optimistic. I marvel at the forces of nature, offering us life in abundance. Yes, they are there if you can see them.

You learn, you grow, you work hard, and you find yourself; and you live life being you.

I'm glad I'll be 85.

Our Helper
By Kelley Benson

"If something's worth doing, it's worth doing well." Do you remember ever being told that? Probably so. It almost seems ingrained in us to want to try to do our best, although many people ignore the tugging at their heart to go ahead and give it all they have. Maybe that's why God wants us to be like little children, because kids can get so excited when they know they've colored their best, threw their best, danced, sang, climbed, flipped, or drew something their best. They just beam with pride and want everyone to see it.

Think back to probably one of the first things you ever read in the Bible: "In the beginning...." It was the Creation account where God displayed to all who were there to see it, "That's good!" Genesis 1 and 2 gives us the account of God's handiwork.

There are several times throughout scriptures where an inspired writer recounts the week God put all His plans into a reality. One place in particular is at the end of the Book of Job, where Job has been pouring out his heart to God in his defense against his "friends'" accusations.

At the end of his deliberation, God answers Job's heart-cry with some questions for Job. He asks, in Job 38:4-7, *"Where were you when I laid the foundations of the earth? Tell me, if you know so much. Who determined its dimensions and stretched out the surveying line? What supports its foundations, and who laid its cornerstone as the morning stars sang together and all the angels shouted for joy?"* God continues with his line of questions, but I believe it's important that we don't read it as words designed to insult Job, but words that express how proud God was of His creation, His design, and His forethought into what He did. There was a purpose in everything He created, even mosquitoes, and therefore what Job was going through had a purpose as well.

Many people throughout scripture, and others throughout history beyond scriptures, have suffered a lot in life, and yet the way God has designed and cared for all that He made brings us comfort when we suffer. Suffering is only recognized as suffering because of the existence of joy and perfection.

James reminds us of God's purpose in trials and difficulties in James 1:2-8, *"Dear brothers and sisters, when troubles come your way, consider it an opportunity for great joy. For you know that when your faith is tested, your endurance has a chance to grow. So let it grow, for when your endurance is fully developed, you will be perfect and complete, needing nothing. If you need wisdom, ask our generous God, and he will give it to you. He will not rebuke you for asking. But when you ask him, be sure that your faith is in God alone. Do not waver, for a person with divided loyalty is as unsettled as a wave of the sea that is blown and tossed by the wind. Such people should not expect to receive anything from the Lord. Their loyalty is divided between God and the world, and they are unstable in everything they do."*

As James says, during difficulties we just need to get a higher perspective on our situation. Perhaps look into the purpose or benefit of difficulties. However, to do that we need spiritual help, which we just happen to get when we become a Christian. God gives us His Holy Spirit to guide, counsel, comfort, and help us see things from God's point of view.

Jesus said in John 14:16-17, *"I will ask the Father, and He will give you another Helper, that He may be with you forever; that is the Spirit of truth, whom the world cannot receive, because it does not see Him or know Him, but you know Him because He abides with you and will be in you."*

Do you realize what a blessing God's Spirit is to our life? His Spirit is asking to control our thinking, our actions, and everything in between. It's not a question if God will give it to you; it's a question of whether you allow Him to control you. Without Christ, you can't have the Spirit; without the Spirit, you won't have a proper perspective on all the blessings and difficulties in life.

The New Testament is clear about when we receive the Spirit, so I encourage you to study it and recognize the need for us to respond to Jesus' invitation in simple obedience because we love Him for what He's made available to us.

Sharing A Hobby
By Ken Lewis

Sharing a hobby with a group of young people can be a daunting, yet rewarding experience. In this particular instance, the hobby was astronomy, and the group was a 5th grade science class. A couple of things in my favor: most people are fascinated by the stars. Plus, for these students, the idea of getting extra credit for peering through the eyepiece of a medium size, amateur telescope made the event much more interesting.

Astronomy, as a hobby, can be as simple and inexpensive, or as complex and expensive as an individual desires. Getting started only requires a relatively dark sky, a star chart (found in most astronomy magazines or newspapers), a desire to become familiar with the seasonal patterns of stars (constellations) that adorn the night sky, and the time to look up and enjoy the wonders that present themselves every night.

A pair of binoculars may be the next step for some, while the craving to explore the spectacles of deep space may invoke others to spend thousands of dollars on large amateur telescopes and accessories.

The opportunity to share my hobby arose during a casual conversation with a science teacher, during a parent/teacher conference. I expressed an interest in astronomy as a hobby...that was all it took. The next fifteen minutes were spent selecting a promising evening, location, and time to acquaint her class with the beauty and wonders of astronomy.

Four days before the star-party, I was invited to introduce the evening's plans to the class, offering personal experiences with the telescope and answering questions. As I stood in front of the class, recollections of my first telescopic sighting of Saturn flooded my thoughts. I recalled gasping at the spectacular image as the ringed planet crept from behind the cutting edge of the lunar surface during a rare occultation (the passing of a celestial body in front of another). Clearing my thoughts, I looked up to see a classroom of young faces peering at me with expressions of anticipation and maybe a little sarcasm. Silence pressed around me, threatening to steal my breath as I looked over the class. Would I succeed in my intent, or fail in an embarrassing display of incoherent babblings and sweaty palms?

"I can take you back in time," I stated, hoping that such a brazen statement would immediately get their attention and interest.

"You can take us back in time?" one of the students responded.

"Sure he can," the teacher interjected, as she turned to give me a smile of confidence. "Remember, because of the vast distances in space, the starlight we see left its origin hundreds, thousands, even millions of years ago."

"For those of you who would like to be involved in this trip back in time, be in the parking lot behind the gymnasium, Friday night at 7:30, and we'll collect some photons with our time machine," I offered. As the students prepared to leave, their excitement and enthusiasm was evident in the chatter escalating throughout the room. The bait had been taken. Now I had to deliver.

***

My mind was a traffic jam of errant thoughts as I prepared for the evening—remember the extension-cord, they're going to ask a question I can't answer, what if no one shows up? Preparation was going to be a key to the success of the event. A list was compiled of every item that I would need. This list was scanned several times for completeness. Several astronomy books were studied to prepare myself for anticipated questions and to review the locations of interesting objects for viewing. These were details that were in my control, and whose outcome I could predict, but there was one nagging question: how do I keep the students who aren't at the telescope entertained? It would need to be something fun and educational.

A celestial treasure hunt seemed to be a good solution to the problem. A basic star chart was created for each student, using the Big Dipper as a pointer to eight other constellations. Each student would also receive a different star chart containing mystery objects, along with a sealed envelope containing a description for the location of a particular celestial object. When a student correctly located their object on the mystery chart, they would be allowed to assist in aiming the telescope and viewing it before anyone else.

I drove to the gymnasium parking lot with nervous anticipation.

Several students had arrived early to help set up the telescope, and hand out the charts and envelopes. As the meeting time approached and final preparations were being made, I glanced up noticing a few stars peeking from their daylight hiding places, and hoped the evening would be a success. These thoughts had barely passed when cars started pulling into an adjacent lot, and students, as well as parents, began to gather.

The evening was more enjoyable than I could have anticipated. Parents enjoyed the star charts and celestial treasure hunt as much as the students, and their questions were just as frequent and challenging. It was rewarding to hear soft gasps of amazement escaping their lips as their eyes pressed against the eyepiece.

As I packed the equipment, I kept glancing at the dark sky, memories of the evening fresh in my thoughts. The stars seemed to twinkle with an excitement, stirred by the "ohs," "ahs," and frequent squeals of joy that echoed through the stillness of the night. Driving from the parking lot, I hoped at least one student was drifting into a deep sleep with images of Saturn's rings, or the wisps of the Orion nebula flowing through their dreams.

Stuffing Envelopes In Your Underwear
By Stephen B. Bagley

I've been looking at self-employment opportunities to help pay my bills, which arrive each month with all the joy of a zombie apocalypse. There are all sorts of selfie-employee opportunities out there. You can stuff envelopes, sell timeshares, do phone sales, actually sell phones, sell foreclosure information, etc. In all these diverse and mostly unbelievable offers, I found a common thread. They all seem to have a line somewhere in their brochures like this: "You can go to work in your underwear!"

Now that made me curious. Other than people who work in Las Vegas, is there a large segment of society who go to work only in their underwear? And is that a goal a civilized society should be working toward?

I think going to work only in your underwear is a good example of casual Friday gone terribly wrong. Just the idea of seeing my former coworkers in their underwear is enough to give me the dancing heebie-jeebies. There's a lot to be said for clothes. Particularly since they cover our flabby, pale, pimply, blemished, scarred, stretched, misshapen, and sometimes tattooed bodies.

Speaking of tattoos, they're not right for me. I can barely manage to date the same woman for more than six months at a time before her sweet, endearing little quirks make me want to push her down the stairs; do you think I want a picture of a flaming skull on my chest for the rest of my life? (Just in case, that's too subtle: I don't.) And don't get me started about that guy who had the entire New Testament tattooed on his body. There are certain places Bible verses should not be, and groins are among them.

If you didn't wear clothes to work, you'd have to fight about the thermostat setting all the time because your office would either be too cold or too hot for different people. You have to worry about sharp objects on your chair piercing your tender skin. And you might learn that hairy-backed Ed in accounting wears Hello Kitty underpants. Once you learn something like that, you can't unlearn it.

Some of the work-at-home brochures don't mention underwear, of course. Those say you can work at home in your sweatpants and/or pajamas. Once again, there's that idea that wearing clothes is a bad thing. Apparently, the work-at-home people are all closet nudists. Remember that kid who always seemed to lose his swimsuit on camp-outs? He's working at home now.

Admittedly, I'm not the person to ask about nudity. As has been pointed out more than once, I'm basically a prude. One friend once told me that he thought I had been born middle-aged. While there is some truth to that, I'd like to point out that, if I ever ran for President of the United States, the media would find nothing racy to report and might be forced to focus on the real issues. Ha ha ha. Yeah, I laughed at the idea of a responsible media, too.

There are at least two nudist camps in Oklahoma. You might be wondering how I know that—yes, you were. When I worked as editor for the Oklahoma State University newspaper, two or three reporters came to me wanting to do a story about the camps. I'd agreed, but they never turned in a story. The camps value their privacy and don't allow interviews or photographers.

Being raised in the country, I know too much about ticks, chiggers, poison ivy, bees, hornets, rabid skunks, etc., to ever want to be naked outside. I think nudists are—and I hope I don't offend any of my family and friends—bonkers. But I'm a prude. And somewhat proud of it.

The other selling point of the brochures is the money. Money, money, money. They say you can make thousands of dollars a week by using their secrets. You can change your life for the better. You can own a fancy car, a huge house, and take fantastic vacations. And all they need from you is your credit card number and its expiration date and security code.

Oddly enough, they won't let you use their secrets and then pay them. You have to pay them first. This seems to imply they don't trust you, but who can blame them? It's hard to trust someone who's sitting around the house all day in their underwear.

Smilie
By Stephen B. Bagley

For the longest time, I didn't realize the power of *smilies*. If you're not familiar with smilies, they're little typographical symbols used in online communications to give an indication of the tone of the message. Like if you tell a joke or think something's funny, you type :-) or :) which look like a smiling face if you look at them sideways. You can even wink by typing ;-). The period after ;-) is not part of the smilie, but you probably knew that, and if not, the rest of this is not going to make much sense. Just know that it's terribly funny. And wise. :-)

I use smilies, of course, but I didn't realize their power until recently. They can negate the most terrible things ever written. Here's an example: *Your opinions stink. Your politics stink. Your parents stink. Your children stink. Your spouse stinks. You are the most stinky person of all the stinky persons to ever walk this earth. In other words, you stink. :-)* Sounds insulting, doesn't it? But that smilie at the end negates all the power of the insult. It's a gentle jest between close friends. Ha ha! And that's a good thing, because I've seen online exchanges that would have led to undying hatred and multi-generational feuds in years past.

Of course, people behave badly on the Net. They say things to other people that they would never dare say to their face. The anonymity and the distance make people much braver than good sense should allow them to be. That's one of the reasons I don't have Facebook friends that I don't know personally. I want to be able to drive to their house and say to their frightened and pale faces, "Now, what were you saying about my parentage?"

Psychologists say smilies are another example of "passive-aggressive" behavior in today's society, i.e. nice to your face, mean when your back is turned. A dog that engages in passive-aggressive behavior is known as a fear-biter. (The next time your neighbor's rat dog attacks your ankle, you can tell it, "Little dog, you're being passive aggressive," just before you kick its yapping behind over the fence.) A passive-aggressive human is known as a Congressman or lawyer.

Southern folk use something like smilies in regular conversation. They use the phrase "bless her/his heart" as their negating clause. For instance, Aunt Lydia Jo will say, "I wish Betty Sue wouldn't wear yellow. She looks like she was fell out of the ugly tree and hit every branch on the way down, bless her heart."

And her friend Hester will reply, "Oh, I know, but her husband is no better. Why, his face looks like five miles of country road after a flood followed by a herd of diarrheic cattle, bless his heart."

A variation of this allows Aunt Lydia Jo to negate the harmful effects of gossip. "I heard Mattie Mary's niece on her husband's side is running around town with the mailman's second cousin's son again, pray for her."

"Oh, I know," Hester says. "That girl's no better than she is, that's for sure. Why, she wears no more clothes than one of my Jacob's hounds and has no more good sense, pray for her."

I've often wondered if the Baptist preacher's call for unspoken prayer requests during Sunday service was to avoid scurrilous gossip masquerading as spiritual concern. Maybe he doesn't understand the true power of those smilies. :-)

Ten Places To Visit Before You Die
By Loretta Yin

There is a list—Ten Places To Visit Before You Die. And then, there is the list—One Hundred Places To See Before You Die. Now I ask you, how many of us can afford the time, money, and energy to do this? Ten places, maybe...

To me, just driving by the main thoroughfare of a city on a tour bus is not how to "visit" a place. You need some time to get to know the place. "Ten Countries in Seven Days" is never my cup of tea. I lived in London, England, for over a year, and never really got to know most parts of that big city.

Now I do have the time to do some of these suggested "visits." And I can manage financially to do so, if I so desire, but I find such trips a bit too exhausting. Ah, advanced age. Life is not perfect.

Let's see. Suppose I have four or five years left for me to travel to some places, what would be my choices?

I have been to the Pyramids and rode the camel. I have shopped at the bazaars in Egypt. I have ridden the elephant in India. I have climbed the Great Wall of China, and visited the Forbidden City. I have walked on the Glacier in Alaska. I have climbed some parts of the great Yellow Mountains. I have been to the Mayan ruins.

I have roamed the streets of Paris and visited the many museums. I have sauntered through the local Saturday markets in the Loire Valley. I have basked in the sun in Umbria, Italy. I have stayed at a great hotel on the Vatican grounds. I have spent days on the Algarve Coast.

I lived in Hong Kong for many years. I grew up in Shanghai, China.

I think I would like to spend a month or two in a farmhouse in Tuscany, Italy, or in Provence, France. I would like to roam the markets, mingle with the locals, be a traveler and not a tourist. Be anonymous in a local restaurant—but, I would miss my home.

I could take a trip back to Hong Kong to see some of my family. Or, I could take a trip or two in the U.S. to see friends.

But, I don't think I enjoy being a vagabond anymore. I would simply stay home and try to discover the beauties around me. I have been overlooking them for many years. There are hundreds of things that I had not noticed before and many places I had not been to, right outside my doorstep.

So let me "visit them" before I die.

The Red Planet: A Pomegranate Explosion
By Martha Rhynes

In the 1940s, Ray Bradbury became a prolific writer of fantasy and horror stories, usually published as "pulp" fiction. A few of his short stories ("The Man Upstairs" and "Homecoming") appeared in elite magazines. In searching for new ideas for stories, Ray often wrote prose poems about life on distant planets. Since boyhood, he had been fascinated by Edgar Rice Burroughs' famous character, John Carter of Mars, and space voyages.

In 1950, a publisher who recognized Bradbury's talent offered him a contract to combine space-story fragments into a novel, *The Martian Chronicles*. The task seemed insurmountable to Ray until he remembered Sherwood Anderson's episodic novel, *Winesburg, Ohio*, and John Steinbeck's use of prose poems as "bridges" between chapters in *The Grapes of Wrath*. "The Red Planet became a pomegranate explosion," said Bradbury, and he completed *The Martian Chronicles* in three months. The publisher marketed *The Martian Chronicles* as science fiction, a new and popular genre.

Ray imagined (romanticized) a beautiful setting on the "Red Planet" with canals and a life-supporting atmosphere, a mythical landscape. Humans in space ships migrate there to escape social and political problems prevalent in the 1950s: civil rights, atomic war, misuse of technology, communism, and environmental pollution. Unfortunately, these migrants bring the same conflicts with them to Mars.

Science fiction writers Isaac Asimov, Robert Heinlein and Arthur C. Clarke admired Bradbury's imaginative short stories, but they found only a tenuous connection with science and technology in *The Martian Chronicles*. Clarke did concede, however, that Bradbury "expanded the minds of millions of readers who didn't realize there was more to the universe than one small planet orbiting a second-rate star."

Actually, only one of Ray's "Chronicles" might be classified as science fiction: "There Will Come Soft Rains." It is the story of a robot-controlled house that self-destructs. Bradbury did not wish to be placed in the sci-fi category because it excluded him from a wider, mainstream market. However, his publisher insisted. Later, he accepted many awards as a science fiction author.

Bradbury met astronauts and scientists at NASA who had read *The Martian Chronicles* and were inspired by it. He also wrote a script for Walt Disney's Space Exhibit: EPCOT Center in 1976. It describes Earth's voyage through space and time. He wrote magazine articles, stage plays, screenplays, television scripts, poetry, ten novels, forty short story and poetry anthologies, and five non-fiction books.

Before he died on June 5, 2012, this "Poet of the Pulps" and "Voice of the Space Age" asked that the following epitaph be carved on his tombstone: "Here's a teller of tales who wrote about everything with a great sense of expectancy and joy, who wanted to celebrate things...even the dark things because they have meaning...just the joy of being alive for another day, and being able to celebrate a particular sense of that day that you didn't celebrate the day before."

Winter Survival
By Tim Wilson

Winter is sometimes the most beautiful time of the year. When the snow falls and the ice builds on the trees, it creates a different picture of our surroundings that we aren't accustomed to. It's especially noticeable in the countryside if you're traveling from one place to another.

This is also the time of year to see wildlife struggling to survive winter's bitter cold until spring arrives. Nature's beauty of true power is given to all creatures big and small, programmed into the DNA of each for the will to survive.

Just to watch some of the wildlife during this time of year is a blessing in itself. These animals survive the bitter cold temperatures—below zero sometimes—without heaters like we have or the luxury of putting on another layer of clothing when it starts to get colder. They don't have supermarkets full of food like we have.

Yet most wildlife will survive the winter to become stronger and smarter in how they survive, knowledge that prepares them for the next winter so their offspring will survive to ensure their bloodline carries on for their species.

Not too many years ago, people lived this same way. With the luxuries we have in today's modern world, we can't relate to how rough our great, great grandparents had it. Think back to only 1776, with no running water in the home, no electricity, no indoor toilets other than night pans, no insulation in the walls or attic, and no gas burning stoves, and the clothing made of wool heavy and bulky. Worst of all, no supermarkets full of food with many choices, and there were no cars with heaters in them to get where you were going. A person mainly walked, took a buggy, or rode a horse in the freezing cold winter to get where they were going.

We've came a long way, America, in the past 250 years. Wouldn't it be a shame to go back to the way our ancestors had to live? And the real question is: could we survive as the animals do now?

5!
By Rick Litchfield

When you use an exclamation point as a mathematical symbol, it is termed a factorial and means in the case of factorial 5, 5!: 5x4x3x2x1. Which, while we are on the subject, equals 1x2x3x4x5. So it may be written: 5x4x3x2x1=1x2x3x4x5. Which I'd suppose makes factorials numerical palindromes.

A palindrome is a word or phrase containing the same letters forward as backward. Regardless of case or punctuation. Such as: "Madam I'm Adam." Or: "Murder for a jar of red rum." Or, my personal favorite, the one about Napoleon: "Able was I ere I saw Elba." Don't get me wrong, I love "Mom" and "Dad" and "Bob" and "Anna" and "Ada" and "Madam in Eden I'm Adam." "Wow!" It's just that I find the one with the history lesson a little hard to beat.

Unless, of course, it's by the factorials.

...6!,7!,8!,9!,...

A Mountaintop Experience
By James Sanders

At 4 a.m. I was jolted awake by my built-in alarm clock. Oh! I forgot again; that is supposed to be an opportunity clock, not an alarm clock. Anyway, I leaped out of bed with the speed of a sloth and stumbled into the bathroom, all the while wondering why anyone in his right mind would crawl out of a warm bed, especially at this time of morning, and then get into a cold pickup and ride for hours over roads, if you could call them that, that would churn butter in ten minutes. All that just to lie, sit, stand or walk on a mountain all day while the rest of the crew went hunting.

By 7 a.m., the guys had scattered over the mountain side and valleys below in hot pursuit of the elusive elk. I believe I was the only one to see an elk all day.

I lay on a narrow ridge between three mountain peaks. Between the two peaks on my right is a small park of high mountain meadow that slopes and narrows to this ridge then climbs to a peak on my left.

By about 10 A.M. the sun had warmed up enough for me to unzip my insulated coveralls. The temperature was probably close to forty degrees, but lying in the sun and sheltered from the wind, I was quite comfortable.

I tried to read for a while, but my mind kept wandering from mountain peak to valley, from distant past to present and back again.

In front of me, to the Southeast is a panoramic view of some of God's handiwork. First, there is a narrow valley squeezed in between the mountains on right and left. Approximately two miles away the valley spreads out, and there beside a stream that laces through the valley floor are the remains of a home site. Whether this is the end result of someone's optimistic dreams or just the work of necessity, I will never know. It does provoke thoughts of the joys and hardships of early settlers though.

Earlier in the morning, three elk cows were grazing contentedly in an open meadow near the cabin or what is left of it. A bull elk that I suppose was spooked by the hunters ran across an open space this side of the cabin and into the timber on the slopes of the mountain to my right.

Now and then the sound of a crow calling to its mate blends with the sound of the wind in the trees behind me. Feelings of peaceful serenity are mixed with a sort of eerie feeling of being alone with nature.

High above a barely visible jet crawls across a cloudless blue sky at the head of a long vapor trail. That plane can go farther in one hour than the man that built that cabin below could have traveled in a month.

Looking out beyond the cabin into the distant haze all you can see is mountains. I know there are valleys, canyons, meadows, and streams there, but I can't see them. I wonder if anyone has seen them all up close. I think God looked down and said, "This looks like a good place for a garden. I think I'll sow mountains in it." And so He did. Thanks, Lord, for sharing Your garden with me.

About noon, I heard what sounded like a whole herd of elk crashing through the trees about a hundred yards to my left. I just saw two or three as they broke through an opening in the pines for a moment then were gone down the back of the ridge.

As the sound of broken branches and pounding hooves faded into the forest below, it reminded me of the dreams of life. Too often, we just get a fleeting glimpse of them before they are swallowed up in the hustle and bustle of everyday living. Dreams and trophy elk have a lot in common—the chances of them walking up to you and surrendering are slim to none. It takes a lot of preparation, hard work, and persistence to realize a worthwhile dream.

A while later two of the hunters came in from the same direction the elk came. They had heard the noise but didn't see anything. We sat and talked about the events of the morning, the other guys came in and we ate lunch. I didn't know beanie-weenies and ham and cheese sandwiches tasted so good. Must be something in the mountain air.

The altitude here is close to 10,000 feet and the air is pretty thin. Of course, no one has to tell you that if you exert yourself at all. I made the mistake of going down hill once. After several stops to get my breath and rest my legs on the way back, I decided that from now on my walking would be around the mountain, not up and down.

In the afternoon, I walked around some, read some, but mostly just enjoyed the view and the atmosphere of the place. Once when I was looking out across the mountains I saw the sun reflect off some object in the distance. With my binoculars, I could see there was a town there. Later I learned it was the town of Westcliffe which is about fifty miles away. The guys came in thirsty and tired from walking in and out of canyons all day. Before we left for home, we made plans to meet the next morning, same time, same place.

As we bounced down the mountain evening shadows crept slowly across the valleys then the ridges. Suddenly, the sun slipped behind the mountain, and all nature prepared for the events of the night. Ahead, a deer crossed the road and disappeared in the depths of the forest and darkness.

A perfect ending for a perfect day.

Growing Up
By Mel Hutt

L akeport has been an important part of my life. It was a very impressive age for me. I have many good memories of that era: 1934-1944.

The Stedman's, Kennitz's, Coulter's, Fink's, Webb Goodell, the Cohn's, Swald's, and so many others I grew to know in my youth.

I spent so many hours at the Stedman's until I went to High School in Chittenango. Pearl Stedman's mother, Vandenburg, was like a second mother. She scolded me as well as her grandchildren. She also would reward me for getting her a bucket of water from the well out front of their house. The reward was a warm slice of homemade bread spread with uncolored oleo, which I liked better than butter. It was a unique pump. It had little buckets on chains that scooped water from the depths of the well and bring it up as we cranked the arm and it emptied into a trough that poured into the water bucket. A dipper hung on the well so if we wanted some fresh water to drink we could go there rather than go inside. I often asked Mrs. Vandenburg if she needed a bucket. After all, the reward was worth the effort. I don't remember that the well ever went dry even in the summer.

We kids frequently played "Hide n' Seek" around the house. The Kennitz girls often joined in on the game as well as Lyle and Claire's two sisters.

The road in front of their house led to Oneida Lake. The road, as it went south across Route #31 went on to Chittenango. Lyle, Claire and I would sometimes ride our bicycles the seven miles up to the movies and back and would swear that we wouldn't do it again. That is until the time. The road across the muck lands where the Sky High farms were located was very lonely at night and very dark usually. One time I ran into the deep ditch that lined each side of the road. These were where onions were grown each year and shipped all over the country. The Coulters were the major owners of that company.

Lyle Stedman, the youngest brother, and Claire the eldest of the lot as well as their two sisters were a big part of my years there. The Kennitz girls that lived across from the Stedman's were Vern the oldest, Joy, and the youngest sister whose name I cannot remember at this time.

We all enjoyed ice-skating on the bay in Oneida Lake in the winter. One night we skated when it was 35° below zero. We didn't know it until we got back to the Stedman house where we had some homemade cookies and hot chocolate.

Claire and Lyle were a large part of my life at this time.

Julia, my mother, encouraged me to attend Sunday school and church. Sunday school was in the morning and usually in an old school house just up the road on Route #31.

Our schoolhouse was a one room just around the bend toward Messingers Bay. It was on the north side of Route #31.

On hot days, we would sometimes sit under the tree in the front yard of the school grounds for our classes. We had a bell in the steeple.

Our heat was supplied by a coal burning potbellied stove.

This building housed the first to seventh grades. Those were great times in my life.

Ice Skating
By Mel Hutt

Much of my childhood was spent as a country boy in Central New York. This was a beautiful part of the state with dairy farms and crop farming alike. Winters were snowy and made outdoor sports more challenging. One of my favorite past time was ice-skating on Oneida Lake.

We lived in Lakeport which was located on the lake. It was a crossroad and had some small businesses, such as my father's grocery store. When the lake froze over, ice fishing and skating were prevalent. After school, we had the chore of cleaning the ice of any loose snow and make a bonfire location with wood supplied by used duck blinds that were used for the fall duck-hunting season. The blinds were constructed from the shoreline brush growth in the marshland in the bay of the lake.

My favorite ice skate was the style used to play hockey with the front of the blade curved up and notched. The notches enable me to stop and twirl along with changing speeds rapidly. I did not jump barrels, but did leave the ice for some distance at a time when I wanted to. We had some races and learned to team skate with the girls.

After an evening of skating, we would gather at my friend's house for some hot chocolate drink that was prepared by my friend's grandmother for us. Homemade cookies were also on the menu as we enjoyed the heat of the wood stoves. I lived a short distance from their house and was ready for a good night sleep in our small apartment in back of the store.

Ironically, years latter I met my wife during a blind date at a skating rink. It's a small world.

My Dog?
By Tom Yarbrough

I found him in the middle of the street. He was just a young thing, chasing crickets under a streetlight. I knew at this particular intersection, his life would be snuffed out by on-going traffic.

I stopped my pickup, opened the door and asked if he'd like to go home with me. He stared up at me with sad yellow eyes and tried to jump up to me but was too small. I reached down and boosted him a little.

Now he's 12 years old, sleeps on my feet on the bed, greets me nearly every day when I enter my workshop, loves everybody in his slow, methodical way.

He will gingerly bump heads with you to say hello. He doesn't eat much but he does want you to get up early as possible and let him out to do his business.

Sometimes strangers to our house are confused by him because, if he has one flaw, it's this: my pet friend isn't a dog; he's a cat.

My First Oklahoma Christmas
By Joanne Verbridge

My first Oklahoma Christmas was one I look back on with fond memories. After a busy year of moving from California to Oklahoma, the year was pretty hectic.

This year Christmas was going to be at my house. My daughter was to arrive a couple days before. Also a few friends and lots of family were coming. I was looking forward to seeing everyone, and expected a great Christmas.

One of my friends asked me if I would mind ordering a fresh turkey. I placed some calls and found where I could purchase one. I told the manager, I couldn't pick it up until late afternoon on Christmas Eve. I had too many trips running to the airport and doing last minute shopping. I was assured it was no problem.

After finishing the shopping, my daughter, Robyn, and I headed the twenty five miles to town to pick up our fresh turkey. We visited all the way to town, catching up on mother-daughter talk. When we got to the market, I asked her to ask the clerk at the front of the store if she knew anything of our fresh turkey. I would go to the back of the store and talk to the meat department. She slowly walked away. I could tell she didn't really want to do it, but I thought it was because she wanted to stay with me.

I was at the back of the store when the butcher came to help me. He went in the back area, when I caught Robyn's attention and signaled to her that the turkey was back here. She started walking slowly toward me. The look on her face was as if she was going to be sick. Her mood had changed from cheerful to serious. I was wondering what was wrong, when I realized what was happening. She thought "fresh" meant "alive."

She approached me just as the butcher came back and said, "He was here a minute ago. Let's go check to see if he's over here."

On our way to "here," Robyn said, "Mom, you really don't need a fresh turkey."

Not missing a chance for a little fun, I added a few more

comments to make her squirm.

The butcher returned, not knowing what was going on, didn't have our turkey. He said to us, "Let me check with the guys in the back to see if they saw him."

In my mind, I knew Robyn was seeing the big turkey running around in the back of the store, hiding from us, knowing his fate.

At this point, Robyn was doing her best to talk me out of our "fresh" turkey.

The butcher returned telling us how sorry he was that our turkey got away from them. The store would like to give me a frozen turkey at no charge.

I could see the relief in Robyn's face. On the way home, I explained to her that our turkey wasn't THAT fresh.

Outhouse
By Joanne Verbridge

Work ethics were instilled in me at an early age. I learned to be honest, work hard, and respect others. Having these standards landed me an unusual job for a woman. I was hired as a route driver for a major propane company. I took pride in my job, as I was one of fourteen women drivers, nation wide for this particular company. I drove for this company almost 13 accident free years.

Every day would be a complete new route. Some stops were three times a week, but others that might have been delivered once a year, thus making the route totally different. There was always something happening. Most customers were surprised to see a woman driver. Of course, I would get the usual comment about, "Do you have a match?" I would act as if that was the first time I have ever heard that comment. Truth was I had heard it hundreds of times.

One particular day that stands out in my mind. It was a normal day. I was making my way to the furthest stop on my route. The delivery was to a rice plant. It was crucial for them to get their propane delivery, as it provided fuel for the dryers and many forklifts to keep the plant in operation. There also were semi trucks picking up and dropping off product. Along the backside of the plant was an alley, just a little wider than the semi truck that would dump their rice.

When I made my delivery, I would have to block part of the alley, as the trucks needed to use the alley too. I tried not to take too much time while making my delivery. I was trying to respect the time of the other drivers. I was finishing my delivery when an impatient trucker tried to squeeze by. I watched in amazement as he maneuvered the big rig on the opposite side of me. I bent down to watch the first part of the truck pass. I couldn't help but think he was going to hit my truck.

Surprisingly he made it through with the first trailer. Now came the second. He had to cut his rig left, putting the back trailer completely out of his site. I watched, being thankful he didn't hit my truck. The back trailer had pivoted around and clipped the outhouse that was sitting there. I watched as the trailer pulled the little outhouse along. It scooted along at least ten feet. As the trailer proceeded going further, it looked like the outhouse was attached. It started to rock back and forth. I knew it was going to tip over, but somehow, someway, it disconnected from the trailer. The truck went on ahead.

I thought about what a mess that could have been and how good it was that no one was in there. I had no more than thought that when the door flew open. A man, whose eyes were the size of saucers, looked both ways. He came out of there fast and ran to the safety of his own truck. I looked the other way, pretending I didn't see him, hopefully giving him a little dignity.

Finishing my delivery there, I had to move forward to make one more stop. Making this stop, the driver that just hit the outhouse, came over to talk to me. He proudly walked up to me and replied, "You didn't think I was going to make it through there, did you?"

I raised my hand, as I was thinking. I wanted to say, "I was worried, but not as much as the guy in the outhouse." But instead, I only said, "No, I didn't."

I laughed all afternoon about that poor man in the outhouse.

Polio Past
By Ken Lewis

Until the age of eight I'd never felt abandoned, but as I sit alone in a wheelchair, somewhere in a St. Louis hospital, I feel as though the world I've grown comfortable in has been crushed and yanked from my grasp. Through my sobs I keep thinking, I'm approximately 500 miles from my rural Oklahoma home, and I'm not sure which way my parents went after their footsteps faded through a door at the end of an unfamiliar hallway.

Twenty minutes earlier I had been sitting with them, as an admission clerk politely shared information regarding my hospitalization and the visitation rules…plus what can and can't be mailed.

"Kenneth will be just fine, Mr. and Mrs. Lewis. I'm sure he'll make friends rather quickly, once he gets acquainted with the other boys in the ward. Also, Children's Hospital will notify you after each surgery," she explained.

I block the word "surgery" from my thoughts with a mental gasp, refusing to imagine the inevitable.

As Mom and Dad listened attentively, my gaze wandered around the hallway, barely hearing any more details of my new, temporary home. After what seemed too short a goodbye (I remember feeling confident that they really won't leave me), I listened as their footsteps faded. I kept my back to their departure, not wanting to watch them leave. I heard a door close…they were gone. At that moment, I began pushing the wheelchair toward the door, not sure where I was going, or what I'd do once I got there.

So, here I sit, in a small vestibule, surrounded by silence, and beyond the walls…strangers. I attempt to make sense of what's happened through a constant flow of tears, uncontrollable sobs, and flashes of the past—a past that introduced my family to polio in 1956. It doesn't seem that long ago, three years, since the virus invaded my home and my body, much like it had devastated so many families during the epidemic of the late 1940s and 1950s. Deep within my heart though, I realize my parents are doing what's best, but any reasonable thinking is erased by my sorrow.

Tears blur my vision, but I slowly scan the room where I sit. It reminds me of a church—a high ceiling, marble floors, and arched windows. It feels cold and unfriendly compared to the home I woke in the previous morning. I hear occasional, muffled conversation through closed doors, but so far no one has come to check on me…I'm thankful. Outside, I notice a couple of birds, hopping and scrambling in the grass. I wonder if I'll ever get outside these walls to smell the fragrance of fresh grass again, or hear the bird's songs.

The longer I sit the more I struggle to recall happier memories that accompanied me to this place…Mom trying to prepare sandwiches in the backseat of our car while Dad maneuvered corners a little too fast, causing her to toss and tumble. He'd time the next turn with uncanny skill, causing her to lean, then roll, once again, into the floorboard amidst sounds of stifled laughter and grunts. We laughed with each turn, but she still managed to finish those sandwiches…or, Dad getting lost in St. Louis, while mom and I exchanged furtive glances. Since I wasn't in any hurry to arrive at the Children's hospital, I was hoping the family would stay lost, but then somehow find our way back home…instead of where I now sit.

A sound from the door to my right makes me look up. I attempt to swallow the lump in my throat and stifle my tears…big boys don't cry. I see a nurse who greets me with an immediate smile. I can't help but return the smile, as I notice her gleaming white, starched dress and matching shoes. A white nurse's cap sits atop curls of brown hair. Her smile gives me a feeling of understanding…at some time in the past she's seen the sadness of other children sitting here in this exact spot. I look down from her gaze, listening to her footfalls as they slow, then pause at the other door. I listen as the door opens, then closes…she's gone.

Once again, my despair seeks refuge in more pleasant thoughts… my dog, Pug, whom I hope doesn't forget me. Mom and Dad, who at that moment are driving home on the same highways that brought me here (I'd later learn that my mother described the drive home from each visit as her "trail of tears"). My neighborhood friends, who will surely miss me, ask where I've been, and when I'll be back.

The sound of a door opening announces another intruder and I lower my head to stare at my hands. I don't hear the door close, but instead, a soft voice inquiring, "Kenneth, would you like to see where you'll be sleeping, and meet some of the other boys?"

The only response I can muster is a nod of my head, acknowledging her presence, and giving in to the fact that I'll be here for a while.

The short journey to the boy's ward is a teary blur of marble floors and unfamiliar faces. The nurse pushing the wheelchair is nothing more than a soft voice, occasionally asking friendly questions, and telling me about other boys I'll meet in the ward. As we near the boy's ward, the sound of laughter and young voices intensifies. The nurse pauses my wheelchair at the entrance, I'm guessing, so I can take in the scope of the room. It's large and rectangular with a high ceiling and globed lights hanging above a wide center aisle that separates two rows of beds. White, metal-framed beds line opposite walls, facing each other, foot to foot. One wall, the one to my left, has windows spaced evenly along its length. The other wall is solid and blank, except for individual pictures that the person occupying that bed has drawn and displayed. I have a feeling the beds that have a window are status symbols and belong to those that abide by the rules, and wait for their name to move up a list. I feel the wheelchair move forward, angling toward a nice, neat bed placed along the blank wall. The activity in the room slowly diminishes. I lower my head, not comfortable with the attention my arrival has generated. I feel their stares, certain they're reliving the moment they arrived. I feel the wheelchair stop beside my bed, and at that moment, I realize they have been in my place…these tears, these emotions.

During the weeks and months that pass, I make friends, as all youngsters do. I slowly adapt to the routine of the ward. I watch with mixed emotions as I witness boys leaving with their parents after all the surgeries and procedures are completed. I also notice the sad and bewildered faces of new patients, boys being pushed to a nice, neat bed. I feel their sadness and newfound loneliness. Several lie on their beds and cry for hours, missing…well, just missing. After new faces are introduced, I sometimes hear sobs in the night. It's a sad time, the night. But, just as each night gives way to a new dawn, the sadness gives way to laughter and newfound friends.

Eventually, we all return home.

Raising A Glass To Janice
By Stephen B. Bagley

I remember Janice every New Year's Eve.

I met her through an online writing course nearly 19 years ago. We became friends. She didn't have many friends; she had a lot of physical ailments and...let's call them quirks. She didn't bathe enough, she loved cats too much, she talked to herself even when around people, she believed in elves and ghosts and aliens, and she would get too close to people when she was talking to them. Mostly she was lonely and lived in her head. She had been physically and mentally abused by her father, who was dead but deserved to be alive and suffering torments. Her mother was a quiet ghost of a person.

Sometimes I found being her friend difficult when she would wander to strange and dark places I couldn't follow, but let's be honest, I have my own list of quirks. I learned to be her friend on the days when she could allow me and to give her distance when she needed it.

She had been ill and was diagnosed with cancer. The pain did a weird thing: it grounded her in this world like nothing else—no medication—had ever done before. She was alert, funny, articulate. The voices in her head were finally quiet.

The cancer ravaged her. She had no money, and the care she received was mostly minimal. I learned my intense dislike and distrust of doctors and hospitals during this time.

One December afternoon, she was particularly sharp and started talking about her life and her parents, what she had hoped for, how life had tricked her at times. I listened as she slowly ran down. She was quiet for a long time, and then she said, "Stephen, did you know that I was in Times Square once?"

I didn't, of course. In fact, I thought she had lived her whole life in Tulsa. "When was that?"

"I was there with all those people," she said. "All those laughing, dancing people. I watched the ball drop. The noise...I was alone." She stopped for a long time. I thought she had fallen asleep, but she said,

"And in all those thousands of people, I turned and saw my old high school boyfriend."

"Wow," I said. "The odds against—"

"He was alone, too," she said. "And he walked over to me, and we kissed forever and ever."

Her voice sounded weak. She was getting tired. I stood to go.

"And we married and had lots of children," she said. "We live in one of those old Victorian houses in Maryland like in Good Housekeeping. We're very happy." She turned her head and looked at me. And in her eyes, I saw that she wanted me to believe that for her.

"I'm glad," I said, trying my best to not cry and not doing it very well. "You're a lovely couple. Love the kids. Alan is so good in math. And Elizabeth is beautiful."

She nodded, smiled, and went asleep.

If this was one of my stories, she would have passed away then, a gentle going away, but this isn't a story. She lived three months more, and the last two were a nightmare. They couldn't give her enough pain medication. She was either unconscious or writhing in pain. Her mother told me that it was a "blessing" when Janice finally died. I guess that's the word to use.

I think of her, less as the years have passed, but every New Year's Eve, I raise my glass to her and her lovely life with the love of her life. They have several children and live in a beautiful Victorian house in Maryland.

The world runs on facts, but we live on belief and hope. Just because a dream isn't reached doesn't mean it's not beautiful and not worth being cherished. Even though I know it's not true, I want to believe she's in Maryland, happy finally. It's as much comfort as I can manage at times.

Remembering New Year's Eve In China
By Loretta Yin

The house was being cleaned from top to bottom. New clothes were ready for the family and the servants—particularly new shoes, since the ground was sacred because of the New Year. Dirt was not permitted to touch the sacred ground.

The kitchen was bustling with activities. All of us were pitching in to help Cook, even me, the eight-year-old 'missy.' Normally, Papa told us not to get into the kitchen so that our clothes would not get dirty by cooking grease, etc. But this was an exceptional time of the year.

My job was to make little Chinese fold-over omelets with fillings. The cook and Mama had set up a small burner for me in one corner of the large kitchen. I was to make a batch of small egg pancakes, filling them with meats, and fold them over to resemble ancient gold ingots. Cook would, then, use them to prepare one of the many, many dishes. Every dish signified 'good luck,' or 'good fortune,' or 'happiness,' or 'long life,' etc.—all things good.

During the first three days of the New Year, fire was not to be built, nor knives to be used. This was to avoid violence and disaster—one of the many traditions we observed.

There were many, many dishes prepared, enough to feed the family, the helpers, and the relatives and friends who happened to drop by.

On the fourth day, after we welcomed back our "Kitchen God," the kitchen would then resume its normal activities.

Happy New Year!

Style

By Gail Henderson

I have no style. That is, I have no intentional style. The pictures on the walls of my house were all gifts. Each one is very special to me, but there is no unifying theme. It's not that I don't appreciate beautiful things. It's just that, like Thoreau, I don't have a driving need to own them.

This is reflected in my personal style, which I call "invisible chic." I dress not to be noticed. I do buy jewelry occasionally but seldom wear anything more than a pair of earrings. I wear my long hair (graying and uncolored) pulled back in an unstylish bun. I gave up the battle of trying to make my hair submit to whatever trend was current. I never won.

Before me, my mother fought the battle.

A beautiful woman, Mother had a real sense of personal style and wanted her daughters to have it, too. Alas, she would look at me, and her shoulders would slump in dismay. I had good features (after I grew into my teeth), but my hair was an abomination. Thick and rebellious, it harbored resentment toward my mother who fought valiantly until I reached my teen years when she handed the standard over to me.

At first, Mother coped with my unruly mop by cutting it off. That's not to say SHE cut it off. Mother seldom touched my hair. In fact, I don't remember her ever combing it. My older sister was responsible for grooming me and my younger sister. (Come to think of it, my hair seemed to behave for her.)

No, Mother took me to a barber. My hair was tamed! Granted, I looked like a boy with big teeth, but my hair stayed put. For six weeks. It grew with a vengeance, and by the seventh week, Mother was defeated until she could get me back to the barber.

I don't remember how long these skirmishes went on, but I do remember when Mother changed tactics. It was no longer proper for me to sport a boy haircut, so we visited a beauty shop, and there my hair almost met its Waterloo. On the other hand, I thought I was going to be beautiful. I was getting a perm! I now know "beautiful" and "perm" are not synonymous. I went from looking like a bedraggled tomboy to a tall poodle.

Sitting through a perm for several hours was not difficult. I rather enjoyed the attention and, oddly, loved having my hair messed with. What I hated was the aftermath. Permed hair requires a lot of maintenance. I became a slave to curlers and learned to sleep while my head was being tortured. My mother was pleased. I looked like HER child instead of something hanging on a far branch of the family tree.

I hated perms, but Mother was relentless until I hit the teenage years and joined my hair in rebellion. I discovered the ponytail, the precursor of my current hair style. I can't say that I don't sometimes wish for a more modern look, a sleek hairdo that frames my face just so, one that says, "Look at me. I am just as stylish as you are." I swear that's when I can hear my hair snickering, "It ain't ever gonna happen!"

Wal-Mart® Cart Pushers Auxiliary
By Gail Henderson

I am a charter member of the Wal-Mart® Cart Pushers Auxiliary. We don't have regular meetings—mostly because I am the only one in attendance. Once, I attended a "real" meeting, but it was still pretty irregular. It was just me and one other person. I didn't catch his name, but he was very passionate about his membership.

The meeting took place one Saturday afternoon in the Wal-Mart parking lot. After I finished transferring my groceries from the cart into the trunk of my car, I pushed my cart toward the cart corral. That's when the meeting began.

The first item on the agenda was "Straightening of the Carts." Before I could place my cart in the corral properly, I had to rearrange the carts left there by non-members. If the corral contains only a few carts, the meeting is fairly short. On this day, carts were at all angles, inside and outside the corral. This was going to be a long meeting.

As I wrestled with tangled carts, Cart Man appeared of the blue. To say I was surprised would be an understatement. I hadn't sent out a memo about this meeting, but there he was, a young Native American with long hair, grabbing carts and yanking them apart with gusto, shoving them into the corral with a great deal of...um...strength.

The meeting seemed to be progressing nicely, but I felt some discussion of the matter at hand would be appropriate since that's what people do at meetings—discuss things.

"Wouldn't it be nice if people would put their carts up?" I offered.

"@#4% people don't care a *&$% about doing what's right. They don't give a %+#^@, the #$*@@&!"

Okay, then. This meeting had definitely been called to order.

He made a few more disparaging comments about human nature, which I can't remember, nor would I have enough symbols on my keyboard to write.

I must have mumbled a few words of agreement. That was the polite thing to do, and it helped me close my mouth which had dropped open in awe of his extensive vocabulary.

The meeting was adjourned as quickly as it had begun. Cart Man disappeared in a cloud of invective.

That was the last (and only) meeting of the Wal-Mart Cart Pushers Auxiliary at which there was a quorum. Mostly, I straighten the carts alone, but I always look over my shoulder to see if anyone will join me. I like to think that young man has meetings of his own, cleaning up the world, one cart at a time.

Winter Time
By Mel Hutt

Our four seasons of the year end with the wintertime. My memories of the snowy Christmases and New Years are both good and not so good.

When our children were young we took them away from their Christmas celebration at home with their presents and haul them off to one of their Grandmothers homes for the dinner and afternoon. This we changed when our grandchildren came upon the scene. We went to their house and enjoyed them showing us their Christmas presents and enjoy a meal at their abode.

The winters of Central New York were real snowy and our kids had a great time in the snow banks and with their sleds. Their stays outdoors were interrupted when the cold hands were brought inside with the wet clothes to be dried and warmed.

Our heating facilities at our house in Oneida were by an oil fired gravity fed furnace. One stormy day we ran out of fuel during a storm as our fuel delivery didn't make it to us and we ran out. Our good friend, who we appreciate to this day, made a trip to get a barrel full of oil for us and we rolled the barrel over the snow banks as our driveway was impassable from the deep snow. Needless to say, we changed our fuel sources.

Our winters in Virginia were quite different. Christmases were not so stormy as to prevent us from visiting our son and his family.

One time we did have such a severe snowstorm that all traffic stopped except me with my chained back wheels on my car I went where others could not. I missed three days of work, however, as the Norfolk area lacked the equipment to handle the deep snow on the streets.

My winters have been good and bad, but mostly good.

A Prayer For America
By James Sanders

Lord bless America again, forgive us of
our all consuming sin. Hold us in your
loving hand. Touch our lives and heal our land.
Please! Lord bless America again.
Lord we don't deserve your graciousness or love.
Or your abundant blessings from above. We don't
deserve your care, or your kingdom in the air
But Lord bless America again.
Let us prosper, give us peace from the
Mountains to the sea, help us spread the
light of Jesus in our land.
And Lord bless America again.

At Last
By Stephen B. Bagley

Not each other's first love
or even each other's second.
We both lived a life before
and carried the scars to prove it.

We did not love at first sight—
life would never be so neat—
you grimly committed to him,
and I determined to stay with her.

How we fell into each other's arms
proved more to be a laugh there,
a shared moment here, a meeting
of minds and battered hearts.

Remember our sweet surprise
when this casual acquaintance
grew into a firm friendship
and fantastically something more.

Not each other's first love
or even each other's second,
but if fate is finally kind
we will be each other's last.

Baker's Dozen
By Rick Litchfield

Do you remember
Surfing dual five two fives
On virtual C: ?

All *Ada* should know
Palindrome's definition
Forward and backward.

Isaac Asimov
and Robert Anson Heinlein
Science Fiction's best

Listen to Tesla
ambient energy may
yet save the planet

Edwin Hubble owes
Henrietta Swan Leavitt
His debt? Gratitude.

Electrons, Protons,
Subatomic particles
Lise Meitner knew.

Winter's eve waxing
Deuterocanonical
Leaves them mystified

The King James Version
And New International
Both the word of God

Write five syllables.
Follow them with seven more.
Then Another five.

Variable stars,
Cepheids ethereal,
Twinkle through the night.

Let us listen to
Howard Zinn and Noam Chompski
If we'd hear the Truth.

Listen to Tesla
Yes, ambient Energy
Really does exist.

Lilith dreams of me
While tossing Eternally
On the Red Sea's shores.

For Duane and Debra Baker

Child's Poem
By Tom Yarbrough

There was a young kid
That fell from a skid,
While riding his skateboard one day.
He dropped his cell phone,
Fell skinned to the bone,
But texted his mother right away.
He lay in the dirt,
While feeling his hurt,
Sent pictures of blood on his shirt.
His mother said, "Son, what have you begun?
You scared me just now
Lying flat in the road,
Cause you are my only son."
"But, mom, my cell
Gave me time to tell
A large dog bone was like a stone.
It lay in my path on the road.
I may be wounded and fell like a log
But what about the poor dead dog?"

Color Me Blind

By Sterling Jacobs

There in the classroom
Surrounded by all her students
The teacher posed a question
Thoughtful yet quite prudent.

"If there was a color
A color that you can see
What sort of color do you think
You would want to be?"

"Color me Red," a young one said
"Cuz I'm so awfully hot
Spewing like a volcano
Encased in magma snot."

"Color me Yellow," said another
"Like sunflowers in a field
To their amazing grace
I do so joyously yield."

"Color me Orange," said another
"Like the setting of a sun
Making peace with the night
Showing stars so big and bright.

"Color me Blue," said another
"Like the splashing swishing sea
So I might swim in its waters
With a blessed, blissful glee."

"Color me Green," said another
"Like leaves in a pile
I could play inside them
For quite a little while."

Then a timid hand was raised
At the back of the facility
From a little boy whose eyes were blind
For that was his disability.

He pondered for a moment
For he was shy and meek
Then an answer formed upon his lips
As he started to speak.

"Color me Black," he softly said
In a tone sincere and kind
Then he followed with a steady breath
"I'm all colors combined."

Dream Metamorphosis
By Martha Rhynes

While dancing a *pas de deux* with Mikhail Barishnikov,
I prance, turn, and leap, and my tutu falls off.
Face flushing, mouth dry, I hear the audience cough;
So I flutter off on gauzy wings, a yellow butterfly.
I sip nectar, meet a Monarch, and flit to the sky.
Swift wings of swooping swallows warn soon I may die.
Zooming upward to heaven, I leave a white jet stream.
Earth below looks like a patchwork quilt with flowing river seams.
Past the silver moon, I follow my star to the end of a lovely dream.

Ice Time
By Eric Collier

Baby's first cry in new mother's arms.
Red and yellow tulips push through snow.
Blue spotted eggs fill grass and twig nest.
Life renews, replenishing by command.
Sing, dance, rejoice for the chance to be.
Seconds melt away like ice in fire.
Climbing tall trees, fast swinging in swings
Gives way to slow walking, cane in hand.
Speeding time soars past faster than light.
Capture these moments before they can
Evaporate like the desert dew;
And others are born to take your place.

Insights From A Saintly Cynic
By Sterling Jacobs

He was a grumpy ole geezer
This much I have been told
Life has made him very bitter
Insolent and old.

Yet while this may be true
I think I can safely say
He had a heart of gold
While set within his ways.

One day we had a conversation
And I asked the question why
Have you become so bitter?"
And this was his reply:

Life's not an even playing field
I'll say right off the bat
It depends on what you're born into
And I'll leave it just like that.

Life is about losing the things
That are most precious to you
And I'll tell you here and now
The losses are more than just a few.

First you lose your innocence
And if that ain't enough...
You lose the charm of youth
And that can be really be quite rough.

You lose your faith in the dignity
Of the creation of man
To view the things that he has done
Is more than one can stand.

And when your body beaks down
It makes it hard to cope
Because if you don't have your health
Then you really don't have much hope.

And when it comes to God
This much I'll surely say
The higher and harder you reach for him
The further he is away.

Yep, life ain't a bowl of cherries
It certainly ain't no picnic
And you can mark my words
Quoth the insightful saintly cynic.

Invitation
By Gail Henderson

Will you come to my funeral?
I will lie in state
inside a covered Pyrex® dish.
My soul will hover near the ceiling
to watch my launching
into the next world.

My children will cry for the mother
they remember, not the old woman
clutching at their lives.
They will cry in fear of their own mortality.
I no longer stand between them
and death.

Which of my guests will be the first to say,
"She was kind" or "We will miss her"
thus beginning the ritual of forgetting?

Will you come and observe
the dance of words performed on tiptoe?
Listen...
Their silences shout the fraudulence
of my existence.

Island In My Mind
By Sterling Jacobs

I was walking by myself
Deep within the park
Then sat myself upon a bench
('Twas' an hour before dark.)

And just a few yards away
I saw him (dressed in slacks)
A man feeding many ducks
All kinds of delicious snacks.

I approached that man
Asking "Sir I...if I may...
Help you feed those ducks?"
He said, "That'll be okay."

We had a conversation
With the time we had to spend
He had an honest candor
One would hope in such a friend.

One could say that he knew how
To really "keep it real"
And this is what he said to me
As we were walking down a hill.

There's an island in my mind
It's a place I've come to know
A retreat from all the angst
All the bitterness and woe.

It's my place of paradise
Impeached of all insanity
Where one can be cleansed
In Mother Nature's sanctity.

It's a place where I appear
When no one else is around
And I walk its path of solitude
With my toes to the ground.

The Island in my mind
Is a place of perfect bliss
And that island is a special place
Very much like this.

I put my arm on his shoulder
And said with no disdain
"The islands you and I live on
Are both one in the same."

Life
By Kelley Benson

If the sunrise is the Morning's glory,
then being born is life's morning.
A child is ushered in with love,
the dreams of life are quickly shaped.
As life blossoms, foundations are built
and hope is formed.
The little life is growing fast.
Thoughts swell and dreams hatch;
of endless adventures fulfilled thru flesh,
Of bold successes to be viewed by all,
"Life is grand" so they say.
And it all awaits the young and the pure.
But the line between dreams
and truth becomes clouded and gray.
As the light of day fades
over the horizon, blending sky and sea,
so does the young man's hopes and dreams:
"Where to go?" "What to do?"
Darkness is where this beast of doubt and fear hides,
Confusing those enthralled in fantasy
"What is real?" the voice will whisper
He lurks within the naïve's heart,
Distorting truth and giving lies.
The hopes and dreams of innocence
become thorns and thistles of life.
The plans have been thwarted, the intentions lost.
Something replaces those thoughts of the young.
Now the beast slyly directs the young man's thoughts,
With his hand on his neck,
he'll guide him down a road unwanted.

But so clever is he that the faded hopes
and deluded dreams are soon forgotten.
What is found instead is no life at all,
But enslavement to another's dream.
One that did not abide with love,
One that never knew the young man's heart.
The beast concealed his awful plan,
And turned the joy of life into something dim.
"What is this life I'm bound to now?
Or am I a slave of some master plan?"
But darkness only lasts so long,
The night's veil will soon be lifted
Giving the sun the glory once more.
The young one's eyes have dreams again,
And hope is now rekindled.
But something's brighter this time around;
The light is bolder, the love is stronger.
The beast cannot hold this dream down.
The dreamer is no longer ruled by the beast.
His grasp will slip as the beams of light
pierce the fading night.
Deeper, deeper this life will flow.
Was he ever really alive? Life was death.
But this death brought new life,
The newness is a revealing start awakened by hope's seed.
Planted deep within the young man's soul.
To know that life is more than a childish dream,
It isn't just sketchy lines of talk and play,
But this living hope guides his life.
The hopes have grown into something taller,
Now mature his plans are wiser.
The beast now knows his days are waning,
His lie will not win this fight,
hope will be born through radiant light.
True life is born yet again.

Light of the World
By Rick Litchfield

A pastiche of passages for those I'm lucky enough to live life loving.

"As long as I am in the world I Am the Light of the World. This is the message we have heard from Him and proclaim to you, that God is Light and in Him there is No darkness at all. Again Jesus spoke to them, saying, "I Am the Light of the World. Whoever follows Me will never walk in darkness but will have the Light of Life." Whoever Loves a Brother or Sister lives in the Light, and in such a person there is No cause for stumbling. Let us then lay aside the works of darkness and don the Armor of Light. In this Way let your Light so Shine before others, that they may see your good works and give glory to your Father in Heaven. You are the Light of the World. A city built on a hill cannot be hid."

Biblical references: John 9:5, 1 John 1:5, John 8:12, 1 John 2:10, Romans 13:12, Matthew 5:16, Matthew 5:14

Lucky Sevens
By Sterling Jacobs

Let me tell you a little story
About old Jackpot Jim
He was such a silly character
There was nobody quite like him.

He liked to work with his hands
He liked to have some fun
"Jack of all trades" is what he'd say
While working in the sun.

And Jackpot Jim (It was just like him)
To have himself a ball
And gamble every now and then
At the local bingo hall.

One day Jackpot Jim
Came up to me to say
Let's go and play the slot machines
I'm feeling lucky today.

Well we went to the bingo hall
So he could play the slots
He placed the highest bet he could
It was a 100 to 1 shot!

He played the Lucky Sevens
Boy! He really was in heaven
Then the most unthinkable thing happened
He won a million and eleven!

Well Jim got wise and walked away
When it was all said and done
He was singing morning glory's praise
For the money he had won.

There I waited a while for him
While he got his winnings cashed
Yet I could see a scowl on his face
He was looking all abashed.

Well he told me what was going on
And gave me all the facts
He could only take 4 dollars home
The rest went towards a tax.

Then Jim went to the truck stop
Forgetting all his regrets
He said "I think I have just enough
To buy me some cigarettes."

My Brother
By Sterling Jacobs

I know you my brother
Though I do not know your name
Yet we're on opposite sides
Of a war that never wanes.

It's a war where bombs
Explode and set fires
And young men grown
Suddenly expire.

It's a war where smoke
Burning black within our sights
Is filled with hate and rage
Mixed with fear and fright.

Now we stare at each other
With guns in our hands
We both pull the trigger…
One falls…one stands.

I knew you my brother
Though I did not know your name
For you'll no longer know war
Its agony and pain.

Then I see something
Hanging out of your coat pocket
Of what appears to be
A silver gold chained locket.

I open it up to see a girl
And what else am I to find
But a little poem scribbled
With these words to keep in mind.

All people as one, this world has gathered
All races of age, it doesn't matter
All fellow cousins, sisters, and brothers
Aren't each worthy to love the other?

Can't we all see the hope and need
To govern this world we live with peace
To protect life's precious path we follow
While keeping our hearts from becoming hollow?

Can't we all take God's advice
And work together towards Paradise?

Not My World
By Gail Henderson

The car radio told me
shareholders lose
when workers eat well,
and women of Colombia
will lose their jobs,
and new factories are cheap,
and profits chase poverty.

Behind the voice,
silence screamed:
You will be punished
for being fast;
you will starve
for the breaks you did not take;
you will watch your children
play in puddles of trash;
you will be just another
sacrifice to the bottom line.

My stomach clenched.
Empathy and guilt did battle
with comfort and distance
as I parked my car in the garage.

Old Booger
By James Sanders

Old Booger was born way up in the Rockies
And worked on a ranch for his keep.
He carried those cowboys, those weathered cow
Jockeys, with pride in his sure-footed feet.
He could stay with a steer through the rocks and
The sage, through meadows, up mountains and down
But as soon as that loop passed his ear, in a rage,
He would plant those sure feet in the ground.
Old Booger could stop and turn on a dime,
He could jerk any steer off his feet.
His color was red, his temper unkind,
Made cowboys unsure of their seat.
Some mornings he was tame as a lamb
And others a wild bucking beast.
Many a cowboy had they been the I AM,
Would have made him a Puppy Chow Feast!

Quatrains Two
By Martha Rhynes

ARACHNIDA

Lonely widow in glistening black,
Spinning her intricate lace,
Guarding her eggs in small white sacs,
On filaments stretched into space.

A scarlet emblem adorns her dress.
Is it the blood of her mate?
First passion, then murder, she must confess.
And weave the web of a black widow's fate.

NATURE
 (Inspired by Ralph Waldo Emerson)

Like hieroglyphs on walls of ancient tombs,
Human history is preserved in silent rooms:
Heroic mind and spirit journeys of the past,
When Nature's strength and majesty seemed vast.

As scientists now probe galaxies in space,
Do philosophers encounter God's omnipotent face?
As microscopes reveal His complex plan,
Do poets still proclaim the destiny of man?

Rain, Rain

By James Sanders

Rain, rain, just what is that?
Does it fall from the sky?
Or is it just some fancy dream
Once told to you and I?
I think I should remember rain,
But oh! It's been so long.
I think it may turn dust to mud
But then I may be wrong.
They say it once had rained so hard
It made dry washes flow
Like rivers in the desert sands.
They say, but I don't know.
They say that lightening streaked the sky
And thunder claps abound.
That lightening strikes would get bright
And crash into the ground.
So God above, our God of love
Who made the sun, the moon.
Who made this earth and gave us birth,
Please! Make it rain real soon.

Reason
By Gail Henderson

When I am sane,
you are the sun
about which I orbit,
my spiraling galaxy,
my expanding universe.

When I am not,
you are a tiny asteroid
plunging into the black hole
of my insanity,
a sacrifice to darkness
that swallows all light.

Nevertheless,
asteroid or galaxy,
you are constant,
solid ground
from which I operate,
sanity about which I whirl.

The Playground
By Sterling Jacobs

I was feeling quite nostalgic
So I decided for a while
To drive to my old school grounds
'Twas more than just a mile

I sat down in an old chain swing
And gazed upon the grass
Then these feelings came upon me
From the memories of my past.

Ring Around The Rosy
On the playground
Slide down the kiddy slide
Ride the merry-go-round.

Climb the monkey bars
Play hide and seek
Recess is an hour a day
While school lasts a week.

Well I went from kindergarten
To middle and high school too
Graduated with my diploma
The future was my boon.

I graduated from college
I had my own degree
I knew opportunities would abound
For a person of my pedigree

Yet soon my eyes had opened
For I would surely learn
Wisdom in this cliché coined
"To whom this may concern"

Ring Around The Rosy
On the playground
Life is filled with compromise
That makes the world go round.

And the Earth is a prison
For the helpless and the meek
And life becomes a guessing game
Regardless of what you seek.

And in this contemplation
While staring into the clear
I saw the World as a big playground
Filled with hope and fear.

Thought
By James Sanders

A thought is a wonderful, glorious thing
that titillates the mind.
But a thought is just a thought
until it's born and then refined.
A thought is a dream's beginning
and with beginnings far behind,
those dreams may blossom like daisies
with glory and riches combined.
So think your thoughts of grandeur,
let them saturate your mind.
But don't expect great riches
to flow from nature's vine.
And don't expect that glory
will be lavished by mankind,
until those thoughts are put to
Work and pass the test of time.

To Jesus
By Tom Yarbrough

You have passed the test of time.
History claims it so.
Never eroding.
Never corroding.
You made your rhyme
Mine.

Vitality
By Rick Litchfield

Lord who loves us hear our Prayer, we thank Thee for Thy tender care. Eternally with us abide, Keep us ever by Thy side. Grant us Wisdom so We'll know the Way of Love You'd have us Go.

God bless the First United Methodist Church, Shady Grove, High Hill, and First Baptist Churches, Life Church, H2O, the Pentecostals, the Presbyterions, Aldersgate, Ada's Ministerial Alliance, Greenville's FISH, and all people everywhere who have any love for Anybody. Let the same mind that was in Christ Jesus be in us, dear Lord. And the same Heart that was in your servant David.

In the Name of the Father and of the Son and of the Holy Spirit
within us.
Amen

What Am I?
By Martha Rhynes

I tip my cap and bow down low
For those who tell me what they know.
Black, blue, red and green,
My marks imprint the sights they've seen.

Across white space from left to right,
Streaks of darkness hide the light.
Red, green, black and blue
I leave a trail both old and new.

Flowing, lurching, large or small,
My rhythmic movements interpret all.
Blue, red, green or black,
I dance in line on front and back.

Although I'm just a simple tool,
Of brilliant minds and sometimes fools,
Green, black, blue and red,
My tracks record what teacher said.

When I Look At You
By Eric Collier

When I look at you, I don't see
Amber locks, nor angelic face,
Nor the poise of a beauty queen,
Nor perfect smile with perfect gleam.

When I look at you, I don't see
Vague wrinkles around hazel eyes,
Nor stretch marks baby left in place,
Nor added years nor added weight.

When I look at you, I do see
The warmest heart I've ever known;
Cuddling new babe in gentle arms,
Comforting child's fears, scrapes, and tears.

When I look at you, I do see
My hopes and dreams reality,
My fondest wishes coming true-
To forever cleave unto you.

Winter
By Gail Henderson

Snow stretches across my interior
like a relentless Currier and Ives.
An incessant veil of white
falls behind my eyes, and
I am blinded by silent ice.

In the middle of me,
the white horizon
will not recall glare of noon,
does not summon blush of dawn,
cannot contemplate indigo of dusk.

No tracks of past or future
impress the endless cold
occupying my soul.
Only the present hauls
its leaden weight
across the expanse of snow.

Never again a flash of red,
a wing against the white.
Never again the whisper
of melting snow.

Bad Day At The Barn
By Don Perry

The old farmer set out to shoe the big chestnut gelding, setting his tools by the stall and leading the horse into the center of the barn where he could work on him. Ol' Jim was a true workhorse some sixteen hands tall and weighed every bit as much as sixteen hundred pounds.

As the farmer began to assemble his tools, Jim stepped back ever so slightly right onto Farmer Smith's foot. The farmer jumped up and down so violently that Jim looked around to see what the commotion was about, shifting his weight to the other foot and thus releasing farmer Smith's foot in the process.

"Yeeooow! My bunion!" screamed Farmer Smith, as he jumped around the barn on one foot while lightly touching the other to the ground in an exaggerated limp.

In ever-increasing circles the farmer limped, and just as he was beginning to slow down somewhat, he stumbled into a giant nest of yellow jackets, causing them to swarm in a huge cloud.

Farmer Smith instinctively stumbled away from the nest, but the damage had been done! Several wasps stung him on the head and shoulders as he limped across the barn, and just as he was passing Big Jim, several wasps zeroed in on Jim's rump. Big Jim instinctively bucked and kicked with both hind hoofs, scoring a direct hit on Farmer Smith's behind.

Farmer Smith went flying out the barn door and landed face down in a large pile of manure. Flies swarmed as he slowly raised his head and looked around.

"Not a good way to start the day" is all he could mumble as he spat out some cow manure.

First Flight
By Don Perry

As I rode my motorcycle through the beautiful countryside, my mind began to escape the realm of natural events and wander over to the fantasy of my upcoming solo flight at the airport where I had been training for weeks to become a full-fledged pilot of the private type. I was due to arrive in some few minutes, but it seemed that I had plenty of time and could afford a bit of flight of the imagination.

Suddenly I was soaring high above the clouds, looking down on lush green hills and valleys, towns and medium sized cities, with lakes and streams on the side, when I decided to practice my 30 degree banked turns, complete with no loss of altitude, just as the instructor had taught me.

"Been raining a little, but what, me worry? Hah!" I hollered to all the world. Looking down at the console, I noticed the altimeter was spinning like crazy as visions of the Red Baron swept through my mind. I pulled back on the stick and easily outmaneuvered him and resumed my practicing those 30-degree turns, thinking no Red Baron can out fly me!

Suddenly, right in the middle of my perfectly banked turn, my front wheel of my motorcycle caught in the grass on the side of the road, causing me to think "Where did grass come from? I'm up here at 5 thousand feet with unlimited visibility." Visibility being a curvy blonde with heavy on the unlimited.

No sooner did I come back to reality did I realize that the grass now slipping effortlessly sideways beneath my tires was in fact the real deal, as Grandpa used to say.

I began praying for traction, which I got as soon as my bike was turned a full ninety degrees to the direction of travel, sliding sideways. This wasn't the desired effect I had hoped for, either.

Luckily, by this time, the bike was only going approximately 40 or 50 miles an hour and not the hundred forty miles an hour at which I had been cruising at five thousand feet.

Off the bike I flew, with a very short flight and making a three-point landing in soft green grass. The three points just happened to be nose, right knee, and left shoulder, nose, right knee, and left shoulder, etcetera, and etcetera.

Oh well, any landing you can walk away from is a good landing I always say. This, on the other hand, turned out not to be one of those kinds of landings.

Later, at the hospital, my wife, Barbara, showed up and the first thing out of her cute little mouth was "Well, Evel Knievel, I see you did it again! Did you enjoy your first flight, Honey?"

Garage
By Stephen B. Bagley

T he dog doesn't miss her. I thought he moped at first, but a few weeks of treats and belly rubs, and Sassy bounces around the house like she had never been in our lives. Sassy's doing better than me.

Her parents picked up her clothes. Some of her belongings, too. They were nice, but distant. If their daughter had been with me longer, maybe we would have become close. They would called me "Son" and made sure I came to visit when she did.

Her mother doesn't hug me when they leave. Just smiles briefly and goes out to their car, clutching an armful of clothes. Her father shakes my hand, but his gaze slides right past me. They have questions. I have no answers I can tell him.

Sassy's betrayal of her bothers me. Aren't dogs supposed to be always loyal? Perhaps he's suffering inside, hidden behind his doggie grin. Or maybe he's putting on a brave front for me and he howls when I'm at work. I don't know. But I doubt it.

Maybe Sassy's smarter than me. She's gone. She's not coming back. He adjusted his worldview. I'm bringing him food and treats. I throw his sopping wet ball so he can bring it back. I pet him and baby him. I let him in and out. She's gone. I'm still here. He's the ultimate pragmatist.

He wants out now. I let him out the back door. I watch him run around the yard. He stays on the left side of the yard. He rarely goes to the right side now. Not since that day. I look to the right. To the garage.

The garage. Where she and I had our final fight. Where things went wrong. When we said the wrong words and did the wrong things. Where I killed her.

An accident, of course. That's what they all say. But it really was. I didn't mean to hit her. I didn't mean for her to stumble back. I didn't mean for those boxes to fall on her.

Because that's what really happened, you know. Yes, she slapped me, and I balled my fist and let fly, but she fell backwards. She didn't keep her balance. The boxes fell. So heavy. And that one box. I meant to catch it; I really think I did. But it might have seemed to someone else that I threw it at her head, but it slipped out of my hands. It was heavy. Filled with old dishes.

The wet sound it made when it hit her. That sound haunts my dreams. I can't forget it.

And it was shock that made me stand there and watch. I was waiting for her to move. I only stood there for a few minutes. Only a few. Then I screamed and threw the boxes aside and held her. I held her. I cried.

I called the ambulance. I cried and shook and yet somehow was able to tell the police that we were cleaning the garage and the boxes fell on her when she was reaching for the one on top. They didn't suspect anything. Really, it was an accident.

I cry. I grieve. I wander around the house. I wonder what her boyfriend is doing now. Does he grieve? Does he suspect? I hope he hurts like I do. I hope he misses her the way I do. It's really his fault. We would have never fought if it hadn't been for him. If she hadn't told me that she was leaving me for him. I got so mad because of him. If anyone killed her, it's him. Not me. It was him.

I hope he's hurting.

Now I sit in the backyard and throw the ball for Sassy.

Over and over and over again.

But never near the garage. Never near where my cheating wife died.

Tomorrow I'm going to burn that garage down.

History, Red Headed Girls & A Dangling Participle
By Don Perry

L
ife as I remember it in the 1950's East Texas was pretty much
a cake walk. Summers were spent fishing for "crawdads" with
a piece of bacon tied to a string, watching little league
baseball, shooting at tin cans with our slingshots or simply hanging
around the comic book rack at Smithers Drug Store, where, for the
large sum of 15 cents, you could get an honest to goodness root beer
float.

Saturdays were spent collecting pop bottles for a refund of two
cents each, to be spent that afternoon at the Ritz Theater. Matinee
shows cost nine cents, popcorn was a dime, and a fountain soda was
another nickel. It was air conditioned at a luxurious 72 degrees. For
25 cents you could live the good life watching Tex Ritter, Lash Larue,
Gene Autry or any number of heroes of that era. My personal favorite
was Lash Larue, who could flick the wings off a fly at twenty paces
with his long, black bullwhip. There were wonderful cartoons shown
before the main matinee, and a serial short featuring Roy Rogers,
Dale Evans, Bullet, and "Gabby" Hayes. Occasionally an episode of
Buck Rogers was thrown in just for good measure. My favorite
cartoon character was Martin the Martian. Needless to say, every kid
in town could be found at the Ritz on Saturday afternoon. It was
"Mayberry RFD, the early years," and most of us were the original
"Opie Taylor." Life in the summer of 1955 was good.

The summer heat of August bore down upon us like a steam bath,
and all were looking forward to relief from the unbearable heat.
Although September would bring the opening day of school, all of us
kids were awaiting it with open arms. Even the local swimming hole
was just a wading pool by then. It was hot! No doubt about it!

That was the year that I was introduced to my evil archenemy,
Mrs. Caskey, my fifth grade teacher. Her basic job was to torture and
demean anyone who did not submit to her particular brand of
learning. I was doomed from the very moment she stepped through
the classroom door. Sideways! The woman was huge! Here was a

woman that absolutely would have won the title of world's largest woman hands down. She could have topped four hundred pounds easily with room left over for breakfast.

As Mrs. Caskey entered the room, an ominous hush fell over the class, and Raymond Kirkland, my best friend, began to whimper, and whine. As she strode toward her desk, she looked directly at Raymond and said "Good morning, Raymond."

Raymond cringed in horror and answered in a meek little voice "Good morning, Mrs. Caskey, ma'am. He sounded as if he were a beaten and forsaken man.

"Raymond, you may have the privilege of introducing your new teacher to the class."

Raymond rose up with the dread of a man condemned to the gallows and stood trembling by his desk. He looked at the floor and muttered in a weak voice, "Mrs. Caskey is my Sunday school teacher and now I have her as my school teacher, too!" He collapsed back into his seat, threw his head down on his desk, and began to sob miserably. After his initial outbreak of emotion he straightened up but hung his head down, looking to see, I suppose, if his manhood was still intact. You could have heard a pin drop in that classroom. Every kid there knew Raymond as brave, courageous and without fear, but in that instant he had been reduced to a whining mass of despair. Later at recess, it was explained to me that she was an original taskmaster to be rivaled only by the Norse pacesetter driving slaves to row across the open sea to England. She was the personification of the classic "fat lady" in the opera.

Mrs. Caskey was to be my English and history teacher. Try as I could, I could never understand the concept of compound sentences and the dangling participle. History simply didn't interest me. What difference did it make that the mountain men wore buckskin clothes and crossed the great Mississippi? It soon became apparent that I would fail both of these classes, and something had to be done.

Next to me sat a girl named Linda McCain. She had red hair, freckles, and wore glasses that gave her the appearance of a large owl. She could have eaten corn on the cob through a picket fence. The most outstanding feature was that she was at least eight inches taller than anyone else in my class and skinny as they come. Linda was also an honor student. I deemed it wise to get to know her better, and soon I was her new best friend. We lived in the same neighborhood, and after school, I would come over to her house and ask if she could help me with my homework. My grades slowly began to improve, but word soon got out that I was the love of her life. The amount of teasing from my friends became almost unbearable. To make matters worse, Linda clung to me everywhere I went, and there was the age-old taunt of "Don and Linda, sittin' in a tree, K I S S I N G" and "Hey, lover boy, when you getting married?" just to name a few. I suffered terribly, but Linda just smiled and tried to hold hands with me. I wasn't having it. I got so mad that I jumped on Ricky Miller and gave him the thrashing of his life. Later, in the vice principal's office, I had to explain what the fight was about, and upon learning the gist of the matter, Mrs. Lansky, the vice principal, smiled broadly and let me go back to class.

Soon after the fighting incident, Mrs. Caskey began to notice that Linda's homework and mine had identical answers and responses. My book report on butterflies was a complete copy of Linda's. I was called to the front of the class and publicly humiliated when Mrs. Caskey informed me that simply copying Linda's report would not suffice. I was handed my book report back with a large F scrawled across the front. Then she turned her attention to Linda, and screamed, "Can't you tell that he is just using you to get better grades, you loon, Can't you see?"

She was obviously losing it. I knew then that it would be war between me and Mrs. Caskey.

My early romance with Linda began to deteriorate as she realized my intent. Oh, she still helped me occasionally, but the romance was now gone, much to my relief. Halloween soon approached. My time with Linda was gone, and my interests turned to other matters such as what costume I could put together, the change of the season to fall, and, now, my revenge upon Mrs. Caskey. My costume was to consist of a plaid western shirt, cowboy hat, and a whip made of rope from the shed out back of our house. I was Lash Larue personified. Halloween night came, and my older brother, who had just turned fifteen, was allowed to drive my dad's pickup to a Halloween party on the condition that he take me along. Here was the golden opportunity I had been waiting for.

We headed to the party just as planned, but it didn't take long for me to convince my brother to go by Mrs. Caskey's house so I could toilet paper it and the trees in front. She lived on a corner lot with no fence around any of the yard, as was the custom in small town USA. As we drove past, my brother noticed clothes hanging on the clothesline in back. Low and behold, there were her bloomers! As I quietly snuck around back and retrieved six of the largest panties in the world from her clothesline, a large cat jumped off the back porch, scaring the wits right out of me. I hastily grabbed every one of those panties and beat a hasty retreat back to the truck where my brother was waiting. The back porch light came as I made a desperate leap into the back of the truck. Later we tied rocks in each corner of those enormous panties and headed out to the courthouse square.

The next morning five pairs of panties the size of a small house were found hanging from the shrubs and trees around the courthouse, but as my dad started out for work he discovered the sixth pair of those panties hanging on the bumper of his pickup. We were both grounded for weeks, but looking back on the whole thing, it was worth it.

No one ever found out who the bloomer bandit was or even to whom the bloomers belonged. No one ever came forward to claim the bloomers, and the incident finally disappeared from the local newspaper, but Mrs. Caskey knew in her heart that I was the culprit. She just couldn't prove it. I'll have to say that the first battle of our little war ended in a dead heat and was a minor skirmish at that.

The next Monday school opened as usual. Birds sang and flowers still smelled fragrant as ever. But that was just the beginning of the next battle.

As I entered the classroom, I spotted a card full of thumbtacks resting by the bulletin board. I used to stick those tacks in the soles of my sneakers and run down the marbled hall, then put on the brakes and see if I could make sparks fly. Never mind that long streaks of stain were left in the marble. I could take one of those tacks between my thumb and second finger, and then snap my fingers to make it spin just like a tiny top. It would spin for as long as a minute or so before losing its momentum and collapsing. While Mrs. Caskey had her back turned toward the class, I spun one of those tacks across the room, landing nicely on her desk. It was whirling beautifully on her desk when suddenly it disappeared off the other side. The whole class was intently watching as the drama unfolded like a cheap comedy, but to my horror, I knew just where that tack had landed.

After completing her writing at the blackboard, she turned around to find me half out of my seat headed to retrieve that tack. She immediately knew I was up to something, but her only reply was "Sit!" I sat like a well-trained Doberman Pincher. She never lost eye contact with me as she slowly stepped toward her chair and sat down. At first she didn't seem to feel anything and continued to look at me suspiciously. Then she addressed the class, and I thought maybe, just maybe the tack had gotten lost. No such luck.

Mrs. Caskey began to squirm, continuing to stare at me and then partially stood up, only to flop back down heavily. Upon seating herself fully, she let out a loud "Whoop!" And jumped up, brushing the back of her dress. Then she said, "You kids read your books 'til I get back" and hurriedly stepped towards the door. As she left, we could see the tack firmly embedded in her backside and lifting her dress to expose stockings rolled thigh high and great folds of skin hanging loosely. Cheers and bedlam broke out as the door closed. Classmates laughed, and even Linda McCain gave me a pat on the back.

She came back about twenty minutes later with the principal in tow. She stepped directly in front of me, glaring with eyes that seemed to glow like hot embers of coal, and proclaimed to all present that I was the cause in some way and that I was going to pay for it. She was hovering over me like a giant blimp ready to rain death and destruction on the target below. Mr. Orr, the school principal, was a little wimp of a man, and he was doing his best to keep her at bay. He had absolutely no effect. After intensive questioning, however, not one student had seen anything. The standard reply seemed to be "Uh, I was reading my book."

No matter how hard I tried to do well in her classes, I just could not rise to her level of expectations. I would be quietly reading and look up to see her glaring at me while I read. If I made the slightest mistake, she was there to see it. I dreaded every day in her classes.

November came and went with the passing of Thanksgiving and I was free for a whole week. Free at last! But as the week ended and school resumed, I knew I was in for a long haul, as my dad the trucker put it. I was moved from the front of the class for safety reasons, even though I was trying to be good. In the end, I was not the one to cause her undoing. Raymond found her weakness and used it against her. Mrs. Caskey was a smoker.

Every once in a while she would set the class to reading an

assignment and leave the room only to return ten minutes later smelling heavily of cigarette smoke. All the class could tell despite the peppermints she used to hide it. This was an offense to be found smoking in the presence of students, even back then.

One day we were notified to report to the school library on the third floor due to our classroom being painted. We were to have Mrs. Caskey's classes in the library that day. As the day progressed, we had her for English and then history. We were to have two whole hours of back-to-back classes with Mrs. Caskey. The library was musty, slightly dark, but quiet. It was obvious that it was rarely used. The wooden floor creaked as Mrs. Caskey locked the door and walked across to address the class. Having dispensed with the English assignment, she quickly assigned a reading of a certain chapter in our history textbooks and disappeared into the broom closet to smoke.

Raymond noticed the key to the library lying on the table next to some books and knew that she had in fact locked the door to the library after entering.

After her smoking break, Mrs. Caskey returned to teach the class, but noticed that the key was missing straight away. She announced, "All right! Who took the key that was here on the table? Where is the key?!"

As the class sat there, she became frantic and didn't notice Raymond as he stepped toward the closet. He slipped in and immediately slipped back out without even being missed. By now, she was definitely losing control and began to rant and scream. Suddenly she noticed Raymond behind her and whirled around with amazing swiftness. She demanded that Raymond tell her where the key was, but he just raised his shoulders with his palms out and said, "Who knows? I don't have it."

Then she whirled around and confronted me. "You! You took it didn't you! You little runt!" About this time, the odor of smoke began to be detected by the students, and someone pointed at the closet that was spewing smoke like a smokehouse. Mrs. Caskey began running around in ever-increasing circles, screaming and searching for the key.

Linda McCain suggested that the key might be in one of the books, perhaps in Moby Dick on the bookshelf. Mrs. Caskey ran to the bookshelf and began ripping books from the shelves, throwing them on the floor after shaking each one violently. Suddenly, the fire alarm went off, and water began spewing foul smelling liquid from the pipes overhead. Mrs. Caskey ran back and forth and screaming for everyone to get out of her way! She was surprisingly spry for a woman her size.

Loud banging was heard at the door, and people began trying to get the door open. Later, it was found that the key was on the floor next to the table. The fire was simply a wastebasket with a rag stuffed down inside. Cigarette butts were found in the basket along with matches.

An inquiry was held by the principal and several school board members. The outstanding question was "Why did you lock the door to the library?"

I am certain that Mrs. Caskey found employment somewhere. Perhaps the local jail? None the less, we had a new teacher who was young, pretty, and always nice and smelled of lilac water. She was the first true love of every boy in the fifth grade, except Jesse Lucas, the meanest kid in town, but Jesse didn't like anything except motorcycles and oil.

Jackalope
By Don Perry

In my younger more impressionable years, about the time I turned eight or nine, I was tutored about the ways of the wild by none other than old Bub Cargil. I could listen to that old codger talk and spin tall tales of his vast hunting and fishing exploits for hours on end. One of the stories he told me was of his hunting Jackalopes out in west Texas.

I pause right here to explain the nature of the beast as told to me by old Bub.

You see, a Jackalope resides in the roughest cactus mounds surrounded by the thorniest blackjack and mesquite trees that can be found. They live in burrows right along with rattlesnakes, horned toads, and Gila monsters. Why, Jackalopes are so ornery that those critters won't even pay them a bit of attention. They are tick-riddled flea bags that, such as they are, they are only good for making chili, not the store bought kind, mind you, but real Terligua pride chili, made with about a five pound bag of jalapenos and two jars of chili powder.

They weigh about 20 pounds soaking wet, that is if you could find any water out in that sagebrush riddled desert. One might confuse the elusive Jackalope with the common everyday jackrabbit, but be not confused. Jackalopes have small antlers just like a deer. A four or six pointer is a rare find indeed. They are ten times more ornery and tenacious than any jackrabbit. They will pose out there just out of gun range waiting for you to get off a shot. Then just as you're about to squeeze off a round and end their miserable life, they will take off around the nearest cactus mound and suddenly appear on the far side laughing their ears off!

Bub told me of the time he snuck up on the blindside of one, no small feat in itself, and after many years of trying to bag one, finally got off a shot. That Jackalope jumped straight up, hit the ground and keeled over graveyard dead. But upon closer examination, all that was left where there should have been a fine bunch of chili makings was only a piece of an ear, a set of scrawny antlers, and a mound of droppings. Apparently, the Jackalope had fled the scene, leaving old Bub a signature present. Old Bub tracked him down and finally got off another shot, ending the critters miserable life.

Years later, I was on my way to Yuma, Arizona, when I stopped in at an old trading post beside the highway. There on the wall was as fine a Jackalope as ever was, complete with horns and everything, with the exception of missing a portion of one ear. Try as I might, I couldn't convince the old coot running the place to part with his fine specimen. He explained that that was one of the few true examples of a Jackalope in existence and how he wouldn't let it go for any price. He further added that his brother had shot it many years ago and it had sentimental value as well.

As I walked out the door in disgust, I happened to ask the man's name.

"Beatle," came the reply. "Beatle Cargil. Why do you ask?"

Shoes For Emily Grace
By Joanne Verbridge

Emily Grace pranced across the freshly plowed field. The clogs of the dirt were painful to her bare feet. She had walked this field many times before, but today in particular she was wishing she had shoes to cover her little feet.

Emily Grace was like most girls; she LOVED shoes! Her only problem was she had too many feet! Emily Grace was a caterpillar! She could never find shoes that would fit. They were always too big, or the wrong color. She would beg her parents for shoes, but they always replied, "One day you will understand why caterpillars don't wear shoes."

In the mean time, Emily Grace would always wonder why? She knew that caterpillars might not wear shoes, but she wasn't an ordinary caterpillar. SHE WANTED SHOES!

She tried on many different types of shoes and didn't realize there were shoes for every occasion. She tried on loafers, flip-flops, sandals, tennis shoes, running shoes, cowboy boots, oxfords, high heels, and ankle boots. There were types that laced up, zipped up and slipped on. What she really wanted now, was a nice pair of slippers.

She would find shoes she liked, but could never find enough of the right size, or when she found the right size, they would be a mismatch of colors.

Maybe, she thought, this was why her parents said, "That she would understand someday."

Emily Grace was so concerned about finding her shoes that she wasn't paying attention to the changes in her body. It wasn't long before some of her feet started to disappear.

Something was happening! She was starting to get wings. With all the changes that happened, one thing was still the same. She still wanted shoes! Now with having fewer feet, she would be able to find the shoes she wanted.

She was no longer a caterpillar, but a beautiful butterfly. She had little antennas, and velvety wings and not so many feet. Her body had changed, but her mind didn't. She still wanted shoes.

She was so surprised when she found the shoes she wanted. The fit was perfect, and the colors were just what she wanted.

The shoes were placed on her little feet. This was so exciting. Finally, after all this time, her dream had come true.

As she started to fly away, there was another problem. Her balance wasn't right. The shoes mad her lop-sided and heavy. She also couldn't get a lift off the ground. She returned the shoes with a disappointed heart. It was now time to go home. She spread her beautiful wings and started flying home, when she smelled something very delicious. The smell was so sweet it was drawing her closer and closer. She landed on a fragrant blossom. The smell was the best thing she had ever smelled. It was at this time, she knew what her parents meant about "understanding."

BUTTERFLIES SMELL WITH THEIR FEET!

That-Boy-That-Died
By Don Perry

I watched as John Little made a long graceful cast out into Pine Needle Lake. John was the best ten-year-old fisherman I had ever met. He would go down to the lake, fly rod in hand, fish for thirty minutes and return with a whole stringer of Largemouth bass, crappie and giant bluegill leaving no time for the shear enjoyment of wading knee deep into mossy water to retrieve his lure or even the chance to slip on the muddy bank as I had tried so hard to teach him to do. How can you enjoy fishing without the mystery and misery of the whole thing? It was obvious that he didn't get the point of the adventure of fishing. I would demonstrate the technique of sliding down the bank and landing in three feet of moss-infested water, but he never would try to imitate the maneuver.

Once when I was making fantastic casts into some lily pads and getting properly hung up, John came by and suggested that I wouldn't have near as much trouble if I could just learn to cast more than ten feet. He then assembled his Shakespeare Supper Cast fly rod and made a long graceful cast of some 45 feet past the lily pads into the clear deep water. I tried to tell him that that would never do, because as everyone knows, the really big ones are up here in the shade of these lily pads.

"They don't like to get the sun in their eyes." I explained. Just as I was about to further mention the fallacy of such a cast, John made a little twitch of his rod tip, and a hole simply opened up where his Double Tufted White Tailed Deer Whatcha Call It Fly had been only an instant before. I watched as he lightly set the hook and brought in a four-pound large mouthed bass.

After stepping out of the pile of lily pads gathered at my feet and walking over to John, I couldn't help but mention that anyone could catch those things. After all, they had a mouth about the size of a garbage can. Why, anyone could hit a target that size and besides, I was after goggle eyed perch which anyone knows have the smallest mouth of any fish. You have to be an expert fisherman to catch those.

I then decided to fish over around the next bend where the water lilies were not so stirred up.

It is here that I should tell you that John Little was a full-blooded Cossotot Indian. He lived on the reservation that bordered the banks of Pine Needle Lake. John was a straight A student, an all-around athlete, was a cub scout, and the best fisherman that I have ever known. As unnerving and irritating as that situation was, I still liked him, but it sure could get on a kid's nerves hanging around someone that perfect. John and I shared the same classes at school and often hung around together after school. My house was just one stop further along the rural bus route than the kids on the reservation. Sometimes I would get off at his stop and sometimes he would get off at mine. Sometimes the bus driver booted us off early by stopping and .proclaiming, "Don and John! Get off my dad gummed bus!" It was these times that built a lasting friendship, not to mention a terrible thirst.

We would finally arrive at his home on the Res., as he called it, tired, hot, and thirsty. His Aunt Thshook had a deep well, and in the summer time, she would lower watermelons down to cool. The water in that well was a cool 50 degrees, and it was this old well that we beat a blazing trail to for cold, clear well water. It never occurred to us that the water was untreated water and had what we called "wiggle tails" in it. Wiggle tails are the mosquito larvae that live in the water until hatching out into mosquitoes. We simply brushed them aside and kept guzzling the cool fresh water. It was a far simpler time, growing up in East Texas.

John coerced me into joining his Cub Scout troop, due to a recruitment drive, and things began to get interesting for me after seeing all the badges and awards that he had. There was a badge for fishing. I could do that. There were also badges for camping, fire starting, knot tying, and various other things. I could start a fire. This I knew because last summer I started a fire that burned up a whole cord of wood and the outhouse to boot; fortunately Grandma made it out of there in time, and no real harm was done. And as for knot tying, I could tie Raymond Kirkland's shoelaces together any time he fell asleep in history class, which was a regular occurrence.

The next Boy Scout meeting occurred the following week at George Sample's house. His mom was evidently the troop leader, which was a bit confusing to me since she had never been a Cub

Scout or even a boy for that matter. She was in the kitchen preparing cookies and Kool-Aid for later. We were in the living room discussing knot tying and the merit badge to go with that. The only knot that I knew how to tie was a hangman's knot, and I began to demonstrate by slipping it over Georges head and drawing it snugly around his neck. George let out a choking sound, stuck out his tongue, which was purple from drinking Kool-Aid, and promptly fell over as if he was dead. His purple tongue had a rather nice effect.

About this time, Mrs. Sample came through the door and let out a shrill scream that caused the dog to crawl under the couch, which was no small feat for a Great Dane and the fact that the couch had half a dozen boys on it. Cookies went flying all across the room, and grape Kool-Aid went everywhere. Mrs. Sweeny ran over to George, ripped the rope from around his neck, and screamed, "My baby!!" This totally embarrassed George to the point he suddenly came back to life and struggled to free himself from his mother's grip. The whole spectacle will forever be etched in George's mind, I'm sure, and I don't believe they ever got the grape Kool-Aid stain off the ceiling. This was the end of my short tenure as a Cub Scout, and no merit badge to boot.

John owned an old beat up canoe that held water much better than repelled it. He would take it out onto the lake and bring back the biggest fish from some undisclosed spot that only he knew about. One Saturday morning, I came over to his place just as he was headed out to go fishing, and he invited me to go along with him.

He asked, "You ever been in a canoe?" as he easily hoisted it up on his shoulders and started off down to the lake.

"Of course I've been in a canoe." I lied. "Oh, I've been in a canoe lot of times, I was a Cub Scout once. All Cub Scouts have been in a canoe before."

John just said "Yeah right, bring the paddles and my fishing rod."

As we headed off down the trail to the lake, I couldn't help noticing that he had the appearance of a boy wearing the canoe like some overgrown hat that had fallen down around his shoulders. When we got down to the lake, John deftly tossed the canoe into the water and turned back toward me as I was trying to catch up.

"Don't hit that branch with the wasp nest on it," he warned.

I stopped and turned around looking for the wasp nest that he was talking about, getting his fly rod tangled in the limb hanging over my head, which happened to be the same limb he was talking about. As wasps streamed out around me, I dropped everything and blazed a new trail in a hasty retreat down to the shore, screaming, "Wasps! Wasps! Make a hole!" as I jumped into the water. John just stood there shaking his head and wondering what to do with me. I said "You got to be fast to survive out here in the wilderness."

As John glanced back toward his house some 50 yards away, he said, "Yeah, right."

After retrieving the paddles and fly rod, we set out in the canoe toward an undisclosed fishing spot, and John began giving me instructions as to how to paddle the canoe. "Paddle on the other side. No, no. Don't sit on the side of the seat. Quit changing sides. Just paddle on one side! No, don't turn that way! Just sit!" We had made it all of 100 yards when I turned to see what he was talking about. John hollered at me, "Don't turn around. Sit down! Don't you know you can't stand in a canoe?"

About this time, water began to come over the side and fill the canoe. I suddenly fell into the water and began to thrash about, trying to get my bearings. Water was all around me, the canoe was floating full of water, and John was in the water on the other side. I could see the shore over about a mile away and began to swim in that direction, but as I swam I could tell it was beyond my reach. The water was cold, and as I turned back toward the canoe, I began to panic. I couldn't make it back to the canoe either, and as I sank into the depths, my impression was that this how it all ends for me.

I woke up on the shore with people peering down at me.

John was kneeling over me and said, "Geez, can't you even swim 50 yards?"

All I could do was nod my head and spit up half of the lake. The ambulance driver loaded me onto a gurney, and I was rushed to the hospital in Crockett. I had to spend the night just for observation, but other than that, everything was going to be fine. The next morning my mom and dad were there to pick me up and I heard my mom say to my dad, "that boy is going to be the death of me."

My dad simply replied, "Only if I don't kill him first."

The next day the news was all over school about how I had almost drowned and all the kids in my class gathered around me with all sorts of questions. "What did it feel like? Were you scared? Did you see God? Was my grandma there?" were just a few of the many questions thrust at me. Being embarrassed to no end, I simply muttered "I don't want to talk about it."

Later that week I got off the school bus with John Little at the entrance to the Res. As we walked toward his aunt's house where he lived, the greeter at the gate waved hello to John and asked, "Who's that with you?"

John turned back to face the man and replied, "This is Don, my friend from school."

The man's face brightened in recognition and he then said, "Oh, I know who that is. That's that boy that died down at the lake."

At this point, it occurred to me that somehow the man was under the impression that I died and came back to life some time later. I yelled back at him that I hadn't died, but had in fact just decided to take a nap.

John looked at me and said, "Yeah, right."

We headed up the road and soon turned into his aunt's front yard, where a large woman stood waiting inside the front door. "Aunt Tshook, this is my friend Don from school," he said as he entered and laid his books on the table.

Aunt Tshook brightened and said, "I know who that is. That's "That-Boy-That-Died."

Again I insisted that I hadn't died, but had only taken a nap after swimming in the lake.

John said, "Yeah, right."

I was beginning to realize that John's "Yeah, right" was not a confirmation of my comment, but an act of sarcasm. Indians had a way of being very subtle about things like that. I never did understand why they were so subtle.

John later explained to me that That-Boy-That-Died would forever be my name on the Res. And that it was an honor for a white man to have the Indian name.

John asked his aunt if I could stay for supper and turned to me and said, "We're having Indian food tonight! "

Visions of a rabbit cooked over an open fire with roasted corn and peppers stuffed with all kind s of things filled my mind as I quickly said yes.

After quickly washing up for supper, we all sat down at the table. His aunt held out her hands toward us boys, and as we held her hands, she asked a blessing on the food and us boys. We then served ourselves heaping portions of a spicy curried chicken and rice with a strange looking squash and a simple salad. It wasn't what I expected of Indian food, but was delicious anyway. Aunt Tshook mentioned that it was a recipe that Mrs. Patel, down at the church, had given her and she had been waiting for the right time to make some good Indian food.

That October the county fair rolled around, and everyone had made crafts of one sort or another. Some entered the pie baking contests, while others had put up their favorite recipe for jams, jellies, canned peaches, or hot chow chow. There were even booths with people selling their wares, such as paintings, handmade quilts, leather products, or jewelry. John and his older brother, Homer, were in charge of just such a booth, operating it for a distant relative named Hector Berryhill. Hector was the local healer on the reservation and as such had great respect within the tribe, but he also made fine Indian jewelry of silver, turquoise, and other stones of several colors. He also did beadwork and leather, but some of the articles were bought locally at Betty's Five and Dime Store.

I was there just as an observer while Homer and John tended the booth and watched the steady stream of people walking past the booth. Just as I was about to leave, a man dressed in a western suit and a big cowboy hat came into the booth and started looking about. He stepped in front of the jewelry case and looked at the things inside. He looked up and asked Homer if he had any Bolo tie jewelry, something like the one he had on, pointing to the front of his neck.

Homer looked at the Bolo, which had a very cheap look about it, and stated flatly, "No sir. We have no jewelry of such fine quality here. We do have some rather nice belt buckles."

Then the man asked, "This stuff made by a real Indian?"

John Little spoke up this time and said, "I think it was made by some old guy out on the Res, you know?"

Homer and John smiled at each other, wise to some inside joke, as the man turned around and spit a stream of chewing tobacco juice out the front of the booth, almost hitting The Honorable John T Whipple's shoe.

The judge stopped momentarily to look at his freshly polished shoes, then looked sideways at the man in the suit and said "Spraying that stuff a little recklessly, aren't you mister?"

The man in the suit just lowered his gaze and said, "Sorry." Then he quickly turned back toward the jewelry case.

It was at this time that I saw John smiling and absolutely beaming at his brother. Homer just smiled and wiggled his eyebrows up and down. The man then turned his attention to a painting of a young Indian maiden wearing a low cut leather dress with beadwork all across the front. The man said, "What you get for this here picture?" while continuing to stare at her well-endowed bosom.

Homer gave John a slight nod, and I could tell something was going on here that didn't readily meet the eye.

John quickly stepped in front of the picture and said, "Oh, that's not for sale, mister. That's the picture of our poor departed mother and we couldn't part with her."

Homer piped in, "We have some fine western shirts over there for a really special price, just $6.99, and that's a bargain, mister."

The man stepped over to the rack of shirts and selected one in his size. He turned around holding the shirt to his chest and said, "What do you think?" at the same time pulled out a twenty dollar bill and handed it to Homer.

Homer replied, "Yeah that one's a real gal getter." Homer glanced up at John and gave him the slightest nod, then proceeded to count out the man's change. John slapped at the painting with a fly swatter, causing the man look up to see what had caused the noise.

John began inspecting the bosom in the painting and glanced back at the man. "Flies! All the time the flies!"

Homer handed the man his change just as a blonde woman wearing a frilly low-cut dress walked in and said in a deep southern accent, "Well, there you are. I was lookin' all over for you. It's time for you to buy me that ice cream now." The man stuffed his change in his pocket and hurried out the front of the booth carrying his western shirt that I had seen on sale at Betty's Five and Dime Store for three for $5.

Homer laughed and said, "That was really touch and go there for a moment. Man, those shirts are so old! The thread is rotten and the first time he washes it, it's going to come out in pieces. And the best part is, I short changed him ten bucks" Homer smiled and said, "Man, am I going to be a good con man or what?"

John just said, "Or what." John later told me he wanted to be a County Judge like The Honorable John T. Whipple. Oddly enough, both boys got their wish.

Several years later my folks moved away from the old place I lived in during my youth, I returned many years later and stopped by the Res where John and I had played as kids. I stopped at the front gate and inquired about going on in. The man at the gatehouse asked if I knew anyone still there, so I mentioned Aunt Tshook's name.

He replied, "If you mean old Momma Tshook, she's still here down by the lake in that old house with the canoe full of Bluebonnets in the front yard. Say, you must be That-Boy-That-Died."

I smiled, nodded at that old name, and stepped back into my car.

As I pulled up in front of the place, I found Aunt Tshook sitting on the front porch. She was now old and frail, but her eyes brightened as I came up the walk. She slowly stood up and began hollering, "That-Boy-That-Died has returned!"

As soon as I got to the porch, she hugged me tightly, saying "That Boy, you came back!" Aunt Tshook was a mere shadow of her former self, barely weighing 90 pounds.

As we sat there on the front porch, we talked of old times and of John Little. "He went off to school and never returned. He lives in Montana now, some big wig, I suppose." Then she pulled an envelope from her apron and showed the letter to me.

It was written on state capitol stationery and was signed beneath the closure of The Honorable John Little Toe Esq. with a simple signature..."John."

The Monastery
By Anna Tynsky

She licks the last bit of cinnamon frosting from between her fingers and slides into the car without spilling a drop of coffee. It is early; she can take it easy and enjoy a long leisurely drive home. She'll be there in time to slap together a sandwich for dinner using up the old lunchmeat if it is still the right color. I shouldn't have eaten that cinnamon roll, she thinks as she secures her coffee, starts the car, and scans the road for Highway 75.

An hour down the road a handmade sign of block letters catches her eye, "Madera Ridge Monastery, Visitors Welcome, 5 miles." Four point five miles later, she decelerates. She hesitates, then exits, the only one to do so. The cars behind her speed by free of impediment. Around a curve and gone, she disappears from the mainstream as if never there.

Sitting within a forest clearing, the monastery is a one story Spanish structure made of stucco and stone. It is the perfect spot to view the distant purple hills, though there are no windows in the building to do so. A tall arch stretches over the entrance. A monk greets her at the door saying little beyond hello. He is a thin man in his mid-50s with the angular face of a thinker; reminding her instantly of her father. With an open wave of his hand, he leaves her free to wander. A sign in the entry reads *"Buscar la verdad, a sabiendas de que cuando se trata"* (Seek the truth; knowing it when it comes). She tries to repress the thought that this sounds like a fortune cookie. Do they make Spanish fortune cookies? To her left and right, dark corridors are lined with wooden doors, closed and quiet behind. Not a single picture or piece of sculpture is displayed, not a single book on a bookcase; no drapery, no rugs or leather chairs give welcome. The bare structure of stone floors and wooden beams above is beautiful in its simplicity; and in this open space, she too begins to feel less crowded and less guarded within.

The monk reappears with a glass of water and asks, "What do you come here for?"

She hesitates. She isn't sure she knows. Should she tell him it was a spur of the moment decision, that she had some extra time on her—

"Many come here in search of God, or come to better understand love," he says.

Now she knows she won't admit the truth. Thinking quickly, she says, "They are the same; God and love; the teaching is that it's the—"

"No," the monk says, "not the same. You confuse them. Love is not God. We search for many things, thinking this is God here and this is God there. Seeking things that eventually break our hearts, and then in time finding something else with the same result. But only one thing will break your heart beyond repair. One thing. And to understand this is what is needed."

This is intense for her. She likes it.

"What? Understand what?" she asks to his back as he has turned and walked away. How annoying, she thinks, these people who give half the answer to what they have spent a whole lifetime figuring out. It doesn't matter though; conversations like this never give peace of mind. A waste of—

"Think about it," she hears from a far corridor.

She begins to pick at herself. "What am I doing here?" she asks aloud. She follows a corridor, which is brightly lit at the end. It opens to a round courtyard with the wide-open blue sky above. She peers out, blinking, and sees a spiral path of red, gray, and black marble rock. A labyrinth. The sun hits the cold stone bringing a Spanish warmth to the old architecture. Exposed to such concentrated light and rare solitude, the stone path is irresistibly inviting. Walk this way, see where it leads, begin with a single step. Unwritten directions pull her forward. She knows she is alone but still she hopes no one is watching as she steps onto the first carved stone. The sun feels good and warm through her shirt as she watches the dust dance ballet-like through angles of light. Step by step she walks the labyrinth toward its center. The courtyard is definitely empty, but she feels intense energy, all around her. Maybe thousands of prayers are circling, she thinks, old prayers, new prayers, weaving together in a swirling song. She has never prayed before, ever, without feeling uncomfortable. She closes her eyes and listens hard as if listening to good lyrics, and then she adds a secret whisper to the fullness.

Sometimes she sees an image in her head of an old woman. The woman sits by a window looking out into a dark evening, waiting and reminiscing. Reminiscing not of her youth, but of peace—peace from the choices she has made through the years. The old woman did not think she would be at this point, alone. Alone, but not sad. Seeing this image now, she realizes that the old woman's face is her own.

She finishes the labyrinth, jumping onto the last stone step as if she is a kid playing hopscotch. She looks back across the steps she's taken. No one to hurry her, no other visitor to break the solitude, it is pleasant here; but she will not last much longer. She feels the strong pull to move on. The car sits gleaming in the drive ready to roll. The edginess to go, go, go, always returns. An ironic life, she is always returning to going.

In the rearview mirror, the monastery retreats to innocuous dimensions. She sees the outside of the courtyard disappearing in the woods, the monk in there somewhere with his veined forehead, the stones unyielding to the elements; all recede away to the elsewhere of memory. The trees beside the road break the late afternoon sun into hypnotic flashes of light and shadow across her face as she drives by. Her thoughts begin to separate and in that opening space between them she thinks about what the monk said, about God and Love not being the same. I have never sought God, she admits to herself. I seek love, always have, and cannot help it. Work that requires my love, waking up each morning in a place I love, finding another to love and be loved: this I have sought. I am simply human. A damned human, I guess. She does not feel broken by this, broken beyond repair. What would that feel like? She begins to feel unsure again, unsure about herself, about what she has learned and accepted as the truth. She feels as if the presence of the lighted courtyard is with her still, has escaped with her.

The road comes to the highway intersection. She waits. The car's good engine idles with a deep purr. It is time to merge again into civilization. Maybe she should go back; return to the monastery and try again. Try again. Try what again? A crossroads confronts her. Go forward, go back, go left, right, make a choice. There is no way to be sure you have picked the true way, and she's never one to be indecisive. "You know it when it comes," the cookie-sign said. She pulls onto the highway accelerating, shifting gears, and changing to the fast lane like a speed glutton. She drives with little concern, as if she'll live forever, as if being in total control of machine and environment, gives her control over fate. She is in the rushing rolling river of modern life once more, taking back conscious choice, her preference for reason, her self-security, her unending resources, her silent God. Tears begin to fall without warning, wetting her shirt.

The monk was crazy, she thinks. All searching—whether God, love, life—all breaks you down. And if you know something is going to break you down, then why do it? Unless, it is necessary. She wipes her face. It is necessary to be broken beyond repair. But this is an old woman's wisdom, she reassures herself. She is not there yet. She may never be. As the daylight fades, she drives, looking out into the dark evening.

Excerpt from *Madison's Journal*
By Stacey Foster

Dearest Journal,
Well, Zane and I were caught by Zell in the horse stable. Zell heard everything we said and saw everything we did.

"I can't believe this! My wife and my own brother!" shouted Zell.

"Zell, I can explain," I told him.

"Just hear us out, please," Zane said.

Zell came up to me and said, "Madison, how could you do this to me, to us, and our babies?"

"I didn't want this," I said, "but it happened, and I fell in love with Zane."

Zell slapped me across the face.

Zane shouted, "Zell! Don't!"

Zell looked over at him. "And you...I can't believe my own brother would do this to me."

"I love her, and she loves me," Zane said.

Zell turned away and walked out of the stable. I followed Zell back to the castle. And Zane did as well.

I went to find my mother. She was in the throne room talking to Kassandar. As I went in, I said, "Mother."

I ran to her.

And started to cry.

My mother asked Kassandar if she could talk to me alone.

I shook my head. "She needs to stay and hear this. She's Zell and Zane's mother. I want you both to hear this from me and no one else."

I told them what had happened. "Mother...Kassandar, I am so sorry about everything. I didn't mean to fall in love with Zane. Please don't be mad at me. Mother, I love my babies; I don't want to lose them."

"Don't worry," my mother said. "You won't." She didn't seem angry, but Kassandar felt differently.

"You have both of my sons in love with you, and now they're fighting over you!" Kassandar snapped.

I looked Kassandar in her eyes. "I didn't want this, really I didn't, but I can't help my feelings for Zane. Please understand."

Kassandar slowly said, "I can see that you do love Zane, more than anything."

"I do," I replied.

She nodded. "Your mother and I will make sure you keep your babies."

Lilly swung the doors open and ran in. "It's Zane and Zell! They're fighting in the library!"

We ran to the library.

Hundreds of books were flying frantically around the room. Most of them hit either Zell or Zane as they used their magic against each other.

I took a deep breath and walked out in the middle of the room. The books paused and then fell to the floor.

"Madison, get out of here," Zane said.

"No," I told him.

"This is between me and Zell," Zane said.

"No," I told him. "It's because I started it with you, Zane."

A book hit my back hard.

I fell into Zane's arms.

He caught me and pulled me up to stand beside him. He looked at Zell and said, "You shouldn't have done that."

"My brother and his slut," Zell said with a sneer.

I started to cry.

"That's the last straw, Zell," Zane growled. "Tonight. Just us. No one around."

Zell smiled.

"What's tonight?" I asked fearfully.

"I want her there to see when I kill you, Zane," Zell said.

"No!" I shouted. "If you kill him, you kill me first."

"You would die for him?" Zell asked me.

"Yes," I replied. "Yes, I would."

Zell shook his head in disbelief.

To be continued in the forthcoming
Madison's Journal
By Stacey Foster

Excerpt from *Ray Bradbury: A Teller of Tales*
By Martha Rhynes

In 1946, Truman Capote, an assistant editor at *Mademoiselle* magazine, discovered Ray Bradbury's short story, "Homecoming" in the magazine's "slush pile." He recommended the story for the Halloween edition. Capote later became the award-winning author of the novella, *Breakfast at Tiffany's*, and *In Cold Blood*, a story about the murders of the Clutter family in rural Kansas. Charles Addams, an artist whose cartoons regularly appeared in the *New Yorker* magazine, drew a spooky Victorian House for the cover of the magazine. The house later became famous as the setting for the eccentric Addams Family of film and television.

"Homecoming" was a tremendous success for Bradbury. It is the satirical story of a Midwestern "clan of vampires, witches, werewolves, shape-changers, and other fantastics," who gather for their annual Halloween reunion. Fourteen-year-old Tim, a foundling, is not like the rest of his family. He has tried to conform to the family's weird lifestyle, but he has no wings, no taste for blood, and he does not like to sleep during the daytime in a coffin in the basement. This theme of being *different* from other members of a family is evident in much of Bradbury's writing.

To celebrate this publishing success, Ray took a vacation trip to Mexico with his friend Grant Beach. Grant's pottery and ceramics business was doing well in gift shops, but he wanted some new ideas, and Ray was interested in stories about Mexico, so they left Los Angeles in Grant's Ford V-8. Neither of them had ever been out of the United States. Both youths lived at home with their mothers, who washed their clothes and catered to their food preferences.

Grant soon grew weary of driving all the time. He wanted to enjoy the scenery, but Ray refused to share the driving chores. Besides being legally blind, Bradbury had a phobia about driving and did not possess a driver's license. As a passenger, he chattered constantly, boring Grant with ideas for new stories and bragging about his recent publishing success. Although they stayed in excellent hotels and inns, the weather was hot, and Grant came down with a sore throat and fever.

People in Mexican villages barely concealed their hostility toward rich American tourists who spoke no Spanish. They were busy cutting weeds and painting cemetery fences in preparation for two important observances: *Dia de los Muertos*, the Day of the Dead or All-Saints' Day, November 1, when they honored deceased ancestors, and All Souls' Day on November 2, to honor *angelitos*, their deceased children. They wore gaudy masks and decorated the graves of loved ones with yellow marigolds and red coxcombs, paper streamers, votive candles, photographs and platters of food and drink. Vendors on the street sold candy in the shapes of skeletons, skulls, and tiny coffins. Ray bought some grotesque *papier-mâché* masks and some carved wooden *diablo* masks, painted with bright enamel.

He heard about a *Dia de los Muertos* ritual that took place on Isla de Janitzio in the middle of Lake Patzcuaro. The night was chilly, but Ray and Grant rented a boat and attended an all-night vigil on the island. Hundreds of participants carrying candles walked from the shore to the cemetery, where they sang and danced, drank tequila, and shot off fireworks.

The next day, the youths traveled to the village of Guanajuato to see the famous mummies. Grant's sore throat was worse, so he stayed at the hotel. Ray walked to the cemetery, where a guide took his money and explained in Spanish that in Guanajuato, families rented the graves in which they buried loved ones. If the rent was not paid, the corpse was exhumed and placed in an underground vault, where the hot dry climate preserved the bodies.

Not knowing what to expect, Ray followed other tourists down some steps into a dark underground chamber. There he saw row after row of dried, naked husks of bodies, fastened by wire and lined up in a standing position. He felt nauseous and faint, but he held his breath and hurried past the mummies to the exit. The experience inspired Ray to write "The Next in Line." In this gruesome story, a cold-hearted American husband deserts his terminally ill wife in Guanajuato, where she becomes "the next in line."

While he was in Mexico, Bradbury received a telegram from his agent who had sold *Dark Carnival*, an anthology of twenty-seven horror stories, to a publisher. Ray could not stop bragging about his success. This annoyed Grant, who resented having to drive when he did not feel well. He insisted that Ray load their baggage, clean the windshield, check the oil and water, and fill the gasoline tank. When Ray absent-mindedly allowed the tank to overflow and gasoline to run out on the ground, Grant exploded, "Can't you do anything right?"

Ray could no longer endure Grant's bad temper and nagging, so he left him with the car in Mexico City and caught a bus to Los Angles. In retaliation, Grant threw Ray's portable typewriter into the river. Later he intercepted an important letter addressed to Ray, informing him that "The Big Black and White Game" had been selected for inclusion in *The Best American Short Stories of the Year, 1946*. Ray would have missed receiving the award if his agent had not made an urgent telephone call. This betrayal ended the friendship between Ray and Grant.

Read more in *Ray Bradbury: A Teller of Tales*
By Martha Rhynes
Available at Amazon, Barnes & Noble, and other retailers

Excerpt from *Tales from Bethlehem*
By Stephen B. Bagley

Now, of course, after all these years, I've heard the tale from other folks. It's plain there be a few misconceptions about the whole happenin' that I, Gregor Nikolas, intends to correct hereforth.

Let me start at the beginning with me being born. Perhaps that be too far back, but I won't bore you with much detail other than to say that I was eighth in my family so it was no surprise when my pater forgot me at Keloe's Inn when I was seven. Keloe has gotten some bad jawing about him due to the events that I am about to relate, but truthfully he wasn't a bad or cruel innkeeper. He washed his plates once a week even if they had been wiped clean by travelers, and made us all take baths once a month whether we needed them or not. Still he fed me and his other workers fair enough and let us sleep inside when it rained or snowed, so we could forgive his unnatural obsession with cleanliness.

That particular night we was full up. His mighty hineyness Augustus Caesar had ordered that all folks return to their birthing place so that they could be counted and taxed. Them Romans be generally good at taxing and at building roads and bridges and have the appeal and personality of old dead, rotten fishes—'specially if those fishes carry swords and spears and be pretty easy about swinging them in the vicinity of other folks' innocent necks.

Anyways, a lot of folks had returned to Bethlehem. Folks usually left Bethlehem when they was old enough to leave since it was a one-donkey town at that time and didn't have much to keep someone down on the farm unless they was just partial to drudgery. Galene, my sweetie except when she's got her temper up and then she don't belong to the gods or any man, said we were going to leave as soon as we saved enough for passage to Rome. Rome was a big city and sounded exciting except for having all those Romans there.

Since folks left town as soon as able, there wasn't much need for lots of extra rooms or inns for that matter. In fact, there were just three inns in town, if you counted ours twice and Nero's Inn of the Seven Seas once. (They served a tasty salad dressing, I hear told.) So we was packed with folks, so much so that the fleas was leaving'.

I was out getting more water to water down the wine. The night was cold and clear. Away from the inn, it was as dark as a soldier's heart. There I got my first notion that somethin' was up. No, really, somethin' was up. A star as it were, shining bright. In fact, as I stood there, I realized it was almost bright enough to read by if those folks who claim to be able to, really can and ain't just foolin' the rest of us.

I got the water out of the well, nearly freezing my hands off, which would have been fairly inconvenient and I'd have to become one of those beggars at the gates. 'No Hands Gregor' they would call me, I'd bet, and then Galene would come and see me and weep at her handsome man and cuddle me and hold me.

The cook yelled at me from the back door so I woke up from my daydreaming and took the water bucket over to him. He half-hearted cuffed me for taking so long, but I'm quick and young and he be old and slow, so he only hit the side of my head and bruised his hand.

I slipped past him and made my way to the common room, which was filled with smoke and noise. Galene was serving ale to some merchants and easily avoiding their hands. She smiled at me and then frowned. She did that a lot. She'd see me and think that she loved me and then see something on me that she needed to be changing, like me washing my hands or getting the manure off my feet. She also had an obsession about cleanliness. I just hoped it wasn't catchin'.

Keloe hollered at me. He was standing at the door, letting in the cold or maybe letting it out. Hard to tell. He was mighty stingy with the firewood.

"Take these people to the stable," Keloe said smugly. "We have no room in the inn."

A man stood there. His clothes were simple but clean. Behind him patiently stood a donkey on which was a woman who was, as they say in the market, with child. Of course, by that, they meant she was going to have a baby, not that a child was with her holding her hand or nothin' like that. I frankly don't understand folks sometimes.

"Follow me," I told the man. I waited until Keloe had closed the door before I added, "Actually, you're lucky. The stable is much warmer and has a better class of rats than in the inn."

The man darted a look at me and then smiled. He looked back at the woman, and he was serious again. She was young and pretty in a quiet sort of way. I led them around back to where Keloe had dug several rooms into the hill to make a place for the animals. We had one empty stall, though.

I grabbed a pole and raked the fresh straw over the area.

The woman gave a little gasp.

"Mary!" the man said.

I realized then and there that she was 'bout to give birth *there and then*.

"Help me," the man said. We both helped his Mary into the stable. I found—no, borrowed clean blankets from some of the packs of the inn's guests and spread them out.

"We need light," the man said. "And water."

I ran to the inn and snatched up an olive oil lamp. The cook tried to stop me, but I ducked under his arm and was outside and back at the stable before he drew enough breath to bellow.

I gave the lamp to the man and then went to get water from the well. I felt a real urgency about this that, looking back, should have surprised me, but it was like the whole night was expectin' somethin'. I felt my heart leap and move in my chest in a strange new way.

I brought the man the water bucket, then backed away from the stable. Overhead the star poured out light like a river of brightness.

"There you are," Galene said. "What are you up to? You have cook so mad—"

"Shhh," I said, reaching out and taking her hand.

"Now, I already told you that you won't be getting no sweetness from me until we're wed so—"

"Be quiet," I said. "Listen. Listen."

She was silent for a few moments and then quietly asked, "What are we listening for?" Her eyes were wide.

The night was still and quiet. The stars whirled above.

"For the world to change," I said, not really understanding what I was sayin' but knowin' somehow it was true.

From inside the stable came a baby's first cry.

Read more in *Tales from Bethlehem*
By Stephen B. Bagley
Available at Amazon, Barnes & Noble, and other retailers.

ABOUT THE AUTHORS

Stephen B. Bagley wrote *Murder by Dewey Decimal, Murder by the Acre*, and the forthcoming *Murder by the Mile*, all in the Measurements of Murder™ mystery series. His other books include *Tales from Bethlehem, Floozy and Other Stories*, and *EndlesS*. He also wrote the full-length plays *Murder at the Witch's Cottage* and *Two Writers in the Hands of an Angry God* and co-wrote *Turnabout*. His poetry, articles, and essays have appeared in *ByLine Magazine, Prairie Songs, Free Star, Nautilus Magazine, Pontotoc County Chronicles, OKMagazine*, and other print and web publications. Visit his website at *StephenBBagley.blogspot.com*. He currently serves as President of Ada Writers.

Kelley Benson wrote *On Target: Devotions for Modern Life*. He is a Christian and small town minister who works to use everyday opportunities to help people recognize how God works in their lives. He is married to his beautiful wife, Jade. They are raising their three young children to see how God should be part of everything people do. He has been involved in the ministry since 1997 in a variety of ministries. A close Christian mentor inspired Kelley to practice "vocational preaching," simply put: to work and preach. This allows him to be involved in the lives of other people in a personal way through secular everyday work while demonstrating leadership in a local church. Visit his website at *KelleyBenson.blogspot.com*.

Eric Collier is a father of two and proud grandfather of six. He started writing poetry for a poetry class hosted by Continuing Education at East Central University, Ada, Oklahoma. He works as a physical therapist at a local hospital. He enjoys camping, hiking, bird watching, and growing vegetables and flowers. His poems were published in *Creations 2013: 40 Ways to Look at Love*. He currently serves as Treasurer for Ada Writers.

Stacey Foster is a writer who lives in Ada, Oklahoma. Her dream has always been to become a famous published author. She was born in California, but moved to Colorado at the age of nine with her parents. She has been writing from a very young age and intends to never stop. This is her first appearance in the Creations anthologies.

Gail Henderson wrote *Red Bird Woman*, a collection of her poetry published in 2013 under the name Gail Wood. She has been published in *ByLine Magazine*, *Creations 2012*, and *Creations 2013: 40 Ways to Look at Love*. She is currently collaborating on another book titled *Bare*, which combines the art of photography and poetry. As a board member for the Oklahoma Department of Mental Health and Substance Abuse Services, she honors the memory of her sister who suffered from bipolar disorder. She holds a Masters of Education in English and Social Studies from East Central University, Ada, Oklahoma. She taught junior high and high school English for 14 years in the small rural school from which she graduated and served as federal programs administrator at the same school for eight years. She loves hiking, digging in the dirt, cooking, and life. Visit her website at *RedbirdWoman.blogspot.com*.

Mel Hutt and his wife have been married for more than sixty years and have three children, eight grandchildren, and seven great grandchildren. When his father died in 1945, he entered the Navy and served more than three years in the Pacific, including Operation Crossroads of the atomic bomb experiments at Bikini. He was then assigned to a destroyer and traveled to places like Australia, China, and Japan, with Hawaii as the stop to and from those places. He shares his memories in memoirs.

Sterling Jacobs received his associate's degree in art in 1999 at Murray State College, Tishomingo, Oklahoma, and received his bachelor's degree in 2007 at East Central University, Ada, Oklahoma. His artistic works center on painting and ceramics and range from pottery to ceramic figures to fine art animation. This is his first appearance in the Creations anthologies.

Ken Lewis has written several articles and short stories of different genres. His interests lie mostly in the paranormal and science fiction genres, but he enjoys exploring other avenues of the art of writing. He is a graduate of the Long Ridge Writers Group, Danbury, Connecticut. He is a firm believer in "Life is learning." His articles, memoirs, short stories, and poems appeared in *Creations 2012* and *Creations 2013: 40 Ways to Look at Love*. He currently serves as Vice-President for Ada Writers.

Rick Litchfield's poetry appears in *A Surrender to the Moon, The International Who's Who in Poetry, Timeless Voices, The Best Poems and Poets of 2007, Creations 2012,* and *Creations 2013: 40 Ways to Look at Love.* He is working on *Shards of Wit and Wisdom: Stories and Stained Glass.*

Don Perry grew up outside of Crockett, Texas, and later moved to Fort Worth. After many years in the aviation field, he retired and moved to a farm outside of Ada, Oklahoma. Don married Barbara Burleson in 1965, has two children, Melissa and James, and three grandsons. Since his retirement, he writes short stories of life and times during his youth, geared toward the young adult and teenaged audiences. Many of his short stories show the humorous and whimsical side of the 1950s life and are often autobiographical in nature. He is currently writing a novel in the Western genre.

Martha Rhynes, a retired teacher, began her writing career by researching the lives of American authors and writing biographies and analyses of their work for inclusion in literary encyclopedias. Her book-length biographies include, *I, Too, Sing America, The Story of Langston Hughes*; *Gwendolyn Brooks, Poet from Chicago*; *Ralph Ellison: Author of Invisible Man*; *Jack London: Writer of Adventure*; and *Ray Bradbury: Teller of Tales.* Her works of fiction include numerous short stories and three novels: *Secret of the Pack Rat's Nest*; *The War Bride*; and *Man on First.* Her non-fiction includes an eBook for young adults: *How to Write Scary Stories.* Rhynes is the mother of six adult children and many grandchildren. Her family operates a cattle ranch in Oklahoma.

James Sanders is the firstborn of seventeen children. He and his wife Charlene live north of Ada, Oklahoma, about two miles from where he was born. He served with the Oklahoma National Guard, 45th Division in the Korean Conflict. He graduated from Oklahoma A&M Tech in electronics and is a retired dairy farmer. In the winter of 1961-62 in a cotton patch near Palo Verde, Arizona, God saved his soul. He is a dedicated Sunday School teacher. He received the Golden Poet Award in 1985, 1987, 1989, and 1990. *High and Lifted Up*, his first book of poetry, was published by Spirit Publications. This is his first appearance in the Creations anthologies.

Anna Tynsky wrote her first poem in high school about the feeling and sound of a perfect jump shot. In college, an interest in the arts increased, especially studies in dance and music, "...finding ideas that connect lives through story, sound, and movement." She is inspired by the writings of Annie Dillard, Joseph Conrad, Emily Dickinson, and contemporary cross-disciplinary artists like Meredith Monk. "The Monastery" is her first short story in print. This is her first appearance in the Creations anthologies.

Joanne Verbridge was born in Oakland, California, spending her life experiences in Northern California. Family brought her to Oklahoma where she enjoys taking time to write about those experiences. She is trying to inspire her young nieces to take an interest in story telling and writing. Her memoirs and short stories appear in *Creations 2012* and *Creations 2013: 40 Ways to Look at Love*. She currently serves as Secretary for Ada Writers.

Tim Wilson is a steadfast believer in truth, justice, and the American way of life, and writes to make a difference by helping others with his hard-earned knowledge and life experiences so others may not suffer the same tragic consequences. He is currently writing a non-fiction book, *Yet to be Disclosed*, based on facts that explain the truth, the whole truth, and nothing but the truth about modern society.

Tom Yarbrough is the author of four books, three non-fiction and one fiction. He is currently editing two works accepted by a publisher. After a long career in counseling and education, he now spends his time with full time writing, family concerns, and hobbies like Rendezvous (an 1840 living history camp) and making bookmarks called "Shepherd Staffs."

Loretta Yin, a retired Realtor and one-time librarian, was born and raised in China. She holds degrees in English literature from the University of Hong Kong, Hong Kong, and the University of Edinburgh, Edinburgh, Scotland. Immigrating to the United States in 1959, she became an U.S. citizen in 1965. She has resided in Ada, Oklahoma, since 1966. Since retirement, she has pursued her lifelong love of art and literature. She is a member of Ada Artists Association. This is her first appearance in the Creations anthologies.